Divorcing Daddy

Other books by Susan Trott:

The Exception
Pursued by the Crooked Man
Sightings
Don't Tell Laura
Incognito
When Your Lover Leaves . . .
The Housewife and the Assassin

SUSAN TROTT

Divorcing Daddy

Carroll & Graf Publishers, Inc.
New York

2164185

Copyright © 1992 by Susan Trott

First Carroll & Graf edition 1992

Carroll & Graf Publishers, Inc.
260 Fifth Avenue
New York, NY 10001

Library of Congress Cataloging-in-Publication Data

Trott, Susan.
    Divorcing Daddy / by Susan Trott. — 1st Carroll & Graf ed.
      p.   cm.
    ISBN 0-88184-754-2 : $18.95
    I. Title.
  PS3570.R594D5   1992
  813'.54—dc20   91-28425
                                                      CIP

Manufactured in the United States of America

To Emery Mitchell and Hughes Ryan
who have just become daughters' fathers.

ONE

I live a life of deceit. My roommate thinks I have a job and I don't. I get up in the morning and pretend to go to work. I throw on my clothes, grab a bite to eat, a swallow of coffee, and am out the door before Nancy is. Then I skulk around until she leaves the apartment, whereupon I skulk back in. I work on my novel all morning, job-hunt in the afternoon, write again in the evening.

I've been in San Francisco two weeks now and I've tried and tried to find work. In another week it will be rent time and then she'll know the truth. Unless I can borrow some money from a family friend I know out here. My idea was to look Lily up when I was settled with a job and she'd be glad to see me. My idea wasn't to look her up to borrow money. Bad enough for her to learn that I had dropped out of college and run away from home.

I'd been living a worse life of deceit there, going to one of the most expensive colleges in America, pretending to study when I was really writing stories. I felt I was taking my father's money under false pretenses. So, midwinter of my sophomore year, I dropped out. I told Daddy I wasn't abandoning the life of the mind by leaving college, but was embracing it wholeheartedly by becoming a writer and abandoning all the social stupidities.

"They'll give me an honorary degree in a few years," said

I, "when I'm famous. But until then, would you be willing to give me a little something to go on with, just until I finish my novel?"

"No," he said.

He said if I wasn't doing what he wanted, he would no longer support me. What he wanted was for me to graduate from college. It was, he thought, a reasonable desire for me, one that many daughters would be happy to fulfill.

"There is nothing worse than being an ignorant person," he said, glaring at me, his mustache bristling, a doughty fat man of fifty with thick black curly hair, and me, his wisp of a colorless daughter. We were in the dining room of the Boston house on Marlborough Street.

"You've managed to learn a few things over the years despite your ongoing bad behavior, but college is where you can truly enlarge your mind and it is the only time in your life you can, when you don't have to think about making a living or deal with a husband and babies." His voice was fervent. "All you have to do is study, think, listen, and learn. What an opportunity! It baffles me you won't seize it. It baffles me that you aren't full of gratitude instead of petulance."

I told him why. "I hate school. I always have. I thought college would be different, but it's not. You still have boring assignments. People still expect things of you, things you don't in the least want to do." I told him what Tolstoy had told Romain Rolland when he was following him around wanting to learn from him how to write: " 'If you want to be a writer,' said Tolstoy, 'then write!' No offense, but I'm taking Tolstoy's advice, not yours."

"Who's Romain Rolland?" Daddy queried thinly, puffing on his Upmann cigar and taking a sip from this beastly brandy he likes called Marc de Bourgogne that's made out of the stems and seeds instead of the grapes and which is so strong that I can't get past the strangling fumes to swallow the liquid. If the fumes weren't incarcerated by the tight-ass rim of the snifter, I'd have a better chance.

I was drinking it because I worship Daddy and always try to do what he does—except graduate from college. I even, for a time, tried smoking a cigar with him after dinner, but it always ended with me in the bathroom vomiting. Ever since I was a little girl I would put the paper ring from his cigar on my finger so we could be engaged, and I was wearing one that night that he cut me off without a penny.

"He went on to get the Nobel Prize," I told him excitedly as if it might follow that by taking Tolstoy's advice, I would too.

"Who? Not Tolstoy, certainly. They never give it to any of the good writers."

Oh God! Now I had to hope *not* to win the prize.

"To Romain Rolland," I explained. For a novel about Beethoven called *Jean-Christophe.* I've been reading all the prizewinners for literature. The best discovery so far is Knut Hamsun. There are others who aren't too shabby," I pointed out deliberately. "Singer, B¨oll, Beckett, Camus, Mann, Gide, Yeats . . ."

"Kafka didn't get it." Daddy frowned through the swirling blue smoke. "Or Borges, or P. G. Wodehouse . . ." Now *he* was being petulant.

"Daddy," I beseeched him, "will you help me? I have to write. I don't want to waste any time. I don't need a degree. I'll keep learning. I'll seek out intelligent people and I already read about a hundred books a month."

"No," he said again, as if I hadn't heard him the first time, which in a way I hadn't, believing he'd come around to seeing my side. "I won't help you," he said absolutely, pounding the table for emphasis, dislodging his cigar ash. "And your allowance ceases as of this moment. You're on your own.

9

"You can stay here until spring," he relented, "at which time I am closing the house and going abroad."

It sank in. He wasn't going to help me be a writer. I felt deeply hurt. But, because he was my adored father and a just man, I knew he must be right. This doesn't mean he doesn't love me, I told myself. He's trying to do his best by me. It's me who's letting him down—not the opposite.

So there went my dream of devoting myself to my art, which if I'd stayed in college (free room and board plus handsome allowance) I could have done deceitfully but which I now honestly couldn't as I'd have to work full-time to support myself.

Still, it didn't cross my mind for a minute to go back to college.

I'd never worked, had no skills. I couldn't get an unskilled job because of being partly educated. At one firm, when I begged for a filing job, the manager said, no, the other girls would hate me, "not just because you're obviously privileged," he said, "but because you're so thin."

It's true, all the women working there were fat. Really fat. They all looked like "before" pictures, I don't know why. It probably said something about the job. They looked nice. I didn't think they'd hate me. Thin people are really in the same boat. It is just as hard for a born thin person to gain weight as for a fat one to lose it but our society doesn't understand that, begrudges any sympathy, and instead hands out the envy which is the world's worst emotion and only makes us thinner.

I am normally thin, but at that point I was abnormally thin because of being hungry. I was still in Boston and I wasn't starving because I had friends I could take a meal with or who would take me out on a date to eat but I didn't like doing that—it was using people—another form of deceit. Now that I'd shed college, I wanted to live truly, as an artist, dedicated to my craft.

"The lyf so short," said Chaucer, "the craft so long to lerne."

And money so *harde* to come by. Something I'd never had to think about before.

I decided to try a new city, so, when I heard of a friend taking a driveaway to San Francisco, I hopped a ride. Nancy had been begging me to come out and share an apartment with her, so that was an inducement.

Nancy is so pretty she should be exhibited. As a receptionist in an art gallery she sort of is. But her salary is small for the honor of adorning the place, which is why she needs a rich roommate and my dad is up there in the big-bucks category, at least compared to hers. So she chose the apartment after she heard I was coming, assuming I'd bring lots of money as well as my cheerful disposition.

Upon arriving, I told her Daddy had cut me off. I swore I'd get a job pronto. She became so anxious about it that I pretended I'd found employment just so she'd stop looking tragic.

She got a bottle of champagne to celebrate. Champagne gives me headaches. I've always been a rum drinker. It's good for you as well as tasty. Not for nothing that the British Navy *had* to drink a tot of it each day. I add a squirt of fresh lime to keep off the scurvy. Double benefit. I've been drinking since age fourteen. We writers have to get going on our alcoholism early. I tried heroin, but it didn't do it for me because of the sleazy characters you have to deal with and not really knowing what you're getting or what part of your mind you're losing, maybe a part you need. Even if drugs were legal, I think I'd choose booze. Junkies seem to crash and burn a lot quicker than drinkers.

Deceitful, I swigged away at Nancy's champagne, pretending to enjoy celebrating the job I'd pretended to get.

I yearn for the day when I'll never have to pretend or lie.
I don't believe I've ever had such a day yet and I'm nineteen
years old, going on a hundred.

My mother was a crazy woman. Unlike Daddy, who loves
me a lot, she didn't love me at all. Maybe she was too busy
being crazy. Can you be out of your mind and love people
too? I don't think so; craziness takes everything you've got.
All you can think about is yourself. She did appear to love
Daddy—if love is going into maniacal rages about a person.

Because of her I never could have friends over, for fear of
how she'd act. I would have to make up reasons why they
couldn't come. When she was in the sanitarium for months
at a time, they could come, but then I'd have to make up
stories why she wasn't home.

Of course I could tell my best friends the truth, but once
you tell someone "I hate my mother, I wish she were dead. I
wish I could kill her," they don't want to be your best
friend anymore.

Anyhow, she died on her own. At the sanitarium.
Hanged herself from a tree. Last autumn. Was I glad? No.
Not at all. I was mad and I was sorry. I felt really sorry for
her, an emotion I'd never once felt for her when she was
alive when it might have helped at least one of us.

I was surprised not to feel glad that she was dead. Life is
mysterious and that's one reason I'm a reader and a writer,
to figure it all out if I possibly can. One book I've read that
I think has some answers is the wisdom of Lao-tsu. I don't
understand it but the words seem to shine with truth. I'm
certain that if I can let in the truth, I'll be on my way.

But how to get there.

Not in skulking. Well, maybe in skulking.

I decided to take a stroll along the Marina Green, as it
was such a pretty morning. Since Nancy didn't go to work
in that direction, she wouldn't see me, so I stopped being

furtive, stopped looking anxiously over my shoulder, and resumed my normal carriage.

The Marina Green is a huge mown field that fronts San Francisco Bay and the yacht harbor, overlooks the Golden Gate Bridge, two islands, and, across the bay, headlands and a mountain. I watched a pure white fog billow in the gate like shaving cream out of an aerosol can. Boston never has white fogs; they are gray and you can't look at them, you just find yourself inside them, groping along, peering away. Nor does Boston have predominately white buildings, and pastel ones—instead, they're ancient grimy brick and stone. And the Charles River never looks blue, whereas San Francisco Bay is true-blue colored water like the ocean itself and beyond it are wild hills. You can look at country from the city, look at a wilderness area from a city sidewalk. It's pretty impressive that you can stand in a major metropolis and look at bare hills. It would be as if in Boston you could look across the Charles River basin and see fields of grass instead of Harvard, MIT, and BU.

But I don't go mad for views. We have a summer house in Gloucester on Cape Ann north of Boston and my mother, when she was there with us, and feeling fairly sane, always made such a big deal about "Come out on the porch to see the sun set on the water!"

She got everyone out there: my four brothers, Daddy, any guests around. Except me. That's when I'd pour a drink and go sit in the darkest corner of the living room. If she really loved the sunset, why didn't she just sit and watch it alone? Why did she have to make a party of it? As if it were her sunset. As if she'd been busy working on it all afternoon.

So I walked along the Marina Green, not looking at the view to foil my dead mother. Instead, I looked at the joggers and kite flyers and dog trainers and sailors legging it over to their boats. And as I walked I sang aloud.

I have an ongoing fantasy that I'm a singer, not in a

coliseum like today's singers dressed in jeans, but a night-club torch singer as of yore in a beautiful satin gown, strapless with cleavage, something I'll never have in this life, a singing voice and cleavage to go with it. Along with the gown, my hair is coiffed. I'm perfectly made up. There are three men who play backup—piano, bass, and drum—and we make jokes together and love each other as fellow artists. I have my followers in every city I go to, and my voice is indescribably sexy and melodious.

I sang "How Deep Is the Ocean." I learned these old ballads from Daddy's record collection.

A young man was running toward me. He had gorgeous red curly hair and fine broad shoulders. He ran with big strides, almost bounds. He wore blue shorts, a gray singlet, and red hair blazed away on his arms and legs as well as on his head.

Something about the runner captivated me, and although I'm not one to stare, I almost did, only looking away as he neared me, also cooling it on the vocal as he passed by. Then I turned to look after him—not for any hope of his stopping, but, well . . . why? Maybe because the writer side of me wanted, with one penetrating look, to search out his soul and self, commit him to memory. He seemed somehow unique to me. I felt a connection, as if he were my doppelgänger, whatever that is exactly, sort of a stranger-twin, a soul-shadow.

I turned and he, although still running, had already turned to look back at me!

I am not a woman men look at, being rather faceless and colorless, being unnoticeable verging on invisible.

Therefore I was surprised, and embarrassed (and thrilled) to see him looking back at me.

Then a horrible thing happened. He ran into a lamppost. People nearby started laughing. Except, because he was running, not walking, he hit it hard. It was made out of stone, some sort of aggregate.

What happened was he knocked himself out. He fell to the sidewalk and didn't get up. That wasn't funny. And there was blood all over his bashed-in head. That wasn't funny.

I crouched down to look at him and the next thing I knew I was sitting on the sidewalk with his gory head in my lap, trying not to pass out. It was repulsive. I hoped I wasn't seeing bits of bone and brain amid the plasma. I felt nauseated and faint. I tried not to look at him, looked out at the bay instead, took deep breaths. I could feel a pulse in his neck. I reminded myself this was a person, not just a wound, one for whom I was responsible, even though I hadn't done anything, even though I wasn't pretty enough to cause him to turn.

"Call an ambulance!" I yelled at the gawkers. "The man's hurt!"

Here was a person running happily along, taking his morning jog, and now he was unconscious—a traumatic wound in his skull—and that's how life was. I had a fleeting vision of my mother hanging from the tree . . . like an outlaw.

Suddenly everything seemed meaningless and scary. I felt alone and vulnerable with no one to care if I lived or died or knocked myself out. It was as if this had happened to me. And here I was, miles from home. I was at the other end of the continent and at the east end Daddy was about to close the house and go away himself.

When the ambulance came, I got in with the downed runner.

Since he was jogging, he didn't have any ID, so I checked him into the hospital on my dad's Visa that I was able to sign. When the poor guy came to he could take care of it. Luckily, in my new life of dedication to art and truth, I

15

hadn't trashed the card, thinking there might be an emergency. This was. (I was not going to use the card for necessities. I had my pride. I'd starve to death first. I'd show Daddy. Within three years I was going to get published, get an honorary degree, and not get the Nobel Prize.)

In the emergency room I sat among the stricken and forlorn while he lay on his curtained-off bed, waiting for attention. Bullet and knife wounds and heart attacks came first with the available doctors. Every so often I peeked in on him. His face looked sensitive and sweet for someone so basically brawny, for such a bounding, rust-pelted runner.

Finally, they cleaned and stitched his head and took X rays. He was well concussed, but they thought he'd wake up pretty soon. By evening he hadn't, and I began to think I should alert Daddy about the Visa charge, so I called him and miraculously found him home. "Hi, Daddy, I'm in San Francisco."

"Nice of you to let me know" came a shout of affront.

"Didn't you get my note telling you not to worry?"

"I still worried," he shouted again so I could feel the full atrocity of my behavior.

"Well, I wasn't going to call until I was settled with a job, but as it turns out I still don't have one and I'm calling from Pacific Hospital, where I had to use your Visa card."

"Are you all right?" He modified his voice, concern creeping in.

"Yes, I'm fine." I told him what happened and, like the witnesses to the accident, he laughed. I told him it wasn't funny because the guy had gone into a coma.

"I feel responsible," I said. "Anyhow, since he's nameless, there's no one else to watch over him."

"I think you've done right," Daddy said. "Don't worry about the money." He paused and said musingly, "I wonder why he turned to look at you."

16

TWO

It was eight o'clock but, being April, still light when I walked down Pacific Heights from the hospital to my building. It overlooked the Bay and the Marina Green— although our apartment was second floor back and had no view. It was Spanish-Moorish in design, white stucco with a red tile roof. The entrance sported arches, filigree, and tiles, in the spirit of the Alhambra in Granada, Spain. A fountain and a decoratively tiled bench made a tiny park of the building's garden. On the fountain, neither Spanish nor Moorish but pretty and playful, was a bronze seal, green with patina, spouting water.

My friend, m Gromy, was waiting for me out front on Marina Boulevard. She lived in the neighborhood, possibly in our building. She was a teenager, thin and leggy with black curly hair, blue eyes, and big teeth. She always waylaid me on my comings and goings and talked to me earnestly but incomprehensibly. She seemed to be in possession of not only her own language but her own world. I was always glad to see her because she was the only one I knew in town besides Nancy and my family friend I hadn't looked up yet to borrow money from.

"M Gromy," she said.

"Hi, m Gromy. How are you doing?"

She laughed, repeating "m Gromy" several times, maybe

amused because it wasn't her name but a greeting in itself. As far as I could tell, she understood my language just fine, and maybe my world, so the relationship worked for me. She understood me a lot better than, say, Daddy.

"Fin nd lint," she said.

"Me too. It's been a long and terrible day. I could use a bottle of rum and about three limes."

M Gromy went into a pantomime. She seemed to be imitating me walking. Yes, that could be only my walk. Although . . . was I dragging one leg a little? Did I do that or was this simply a flawed pantomime on m Gromy's part? My walk was my only physical attribute that I was a bit proud of. I liked to think of it as a woman-warrior walk, an I-don't-give-a-shit walk. However, if it in fact included a leg-drag, I was laboring under a huge misapprehension.

M Gromy's pantomimes tended toward the elaborate— she was essentially a tale teller fettered by a foreign tongue —so the next thing she did was imitate the bounding runner. She ran at the nearest lamppost, hit it, and fell down. I ran to pick her up. "Are you all right?" She'd gotten completely carried away and stunned herself.

She regained her feet, looking giddy.

"So you saw the accident?"

She nodded vigorously and started running toward the lamppost again. I grabbed her.

"Cut it out. That's enough."

"Etch," she said grumpily, feeling foiled. "Mrek mrak."

"Well, it isn't funny. The poor guy's in the hospital and I feel to blame. If he hadn't turned to look at me, it wouldn't have happened."

She shook her head back and forth, looking puzzled, probably, like Daddy, wondering why he looked.

Could he have looked because of my leg-dragging? No, don't be silly. That is the thought of a tired person who needs a drink and isn't going to get one, who doesn't even

18

have a dragging leg in real life. Anyhow, it wasn't so much a drag as a hesitation. But that's worse. I don't want to walk in a hesitation step as if I'm perpetually coming down an aisle to the strains of *Lohengrin.*

"Do you think I have a funny walk and that's why he turned to look?"

On cue, she went into my walk and this time the leg didn't drag. But was there a slight mince? Did I have a woman-warrior walk with a mince? There was absolutely no way of knowing for sure until I was rich and could have a videotape made. Unless this could constitute another emergency. Hi Dad, I had to use your Visa again to see if I walked funny. It wasn't for food, mind you, I'm still making it on my own (by not eating). No, I just had to find out if I dragged my leg or minced, thus causing this horrible accident. You started it all by wondering why he turned to look at me. And then m Gromy got me worried. She's my new friend out here, one of those intellectuals I promised you I was going to seek out and learn from to make up for dropping out of college—along with reading my hundred books a month. I've completely stopped reading, by the way. It's hard to read when your stomach rumbles.

M Gromy finished imitating me and I again seized hold of her before she completed the scenario by dashing her head into the lamppost. "I get the picture. I was there."

"Rimphnagel ul ul."

"See you tomorrow. I've got to go in and tell Nancy what happened and explain to her how I lost my imaginary job because of it."

"Manch," she said. "Lachma nd," which probably translated to: Good idea!

Our furnished studio apartment was one large room plus kitchenette and bath. There was a fireplace with a mirror over it and a bay window that had no idea there was a bay

19

within earshot. Here stood dining table and chairs. There were two studio couches and two armchairs and, except for the white ceiling, it was all green. The couch-beds had green spreads, with green throw pillows.

The floor was green vinyl squares with black sperms swimming on them to make them look like marble. The chairs were green Naugahyde. There were two huge plastic philodendron plants flanking the hearth. The landlord was color-blind or fixated. I'm not against green. If it had to be all one color, I'd take green without a whimper. Still, sometimes I felt it might constitute an emergency to Visa some new spreads. There'd been green scatter rugs too, but I unscattered them my first day. It cost seven hundred a month because of the good location and the fancy entrance with the fountain.

Nancy arrived a few minutes after me. "My boss took me for dinner. I brought you a doggy bag. Steak and broccoli."

"Thanks, Nance." (Even the food was green.) "I'm starved."

"There's a loaf of bread in the kitchen. Help yourself."

This was a real meal. I set it out on the table respectfully. Even though the steak was wizened and sicklied o'er with congealed fat, the broccoli repugnantly mushy, I ate with gusto. The sourdough bread was fresh and delicious.

While Nancy closed the blinds and undressed for the night, displaying herself in all her unearthly beauty, I told her about my day and she was mesmerized. "Of course I was late for work," I finished nervously, my eyes darting around the room as they tended to when I was lying, "and when I called from the hospital to tell them I'd be late, they said don't bother coming in, you're fired. But what could I do? I couldn't abandon him."

"Of course not." She began to look tragic again. Not purposely. I knew she couldn't help the expression settling on her face and I loved it that she looked tragic rather than sulky or grumpy as another woman might. "But what'll we do?" she moaned.

"I'll get another job," I promised hectically, "and I'll borrow money to tide me over to the first check," I said, as if nothing could be simpler. It did sound simple in the light of my already having gotten a job once instead of never. Also I'd never borrowed money. I didn't even know how to do it, what to say. I guess one wrote out an I.O.U. Then what? Did one fill it in for any amount, like a check? Maybe the person, him or her (hopefully my family friend, Lily), wrote it out and filled in the amount with a flourish after having generously penned the check. I suspected the paperwork was the least of it and getting the person to agree to it was the crux. Would I have to plead? Would I need a sob story? I refused to have a sob story or to beg. I wondered if m Gromy had money. I knew she'd give it to me with a happy heart if she did, no questions asked.

Nancy was looking in the morning paper under "Jobs Available." I wished there were a loans available section. "Here's a perfect one," she said with false cheer, or maybe it was real cheer. "A writer is looking for an assistant to help him. There's a box number to send your résumé to."

I didn't have a résumé since I was looking only for lowly jobs. What would I put on it? Went to school, traveled summers, bought lots of clothes and books, had servants, made my own bed once or twice, hung up my clothes three times.

"Pays a thousand a month, which isn't a lot, but you'd get by. Go for it. You've got the brains. You can type. You know libraries inside and out. He can't say you're too snooty-looking or too thin. It won't matter. An assistant can look like anyone."

"What do you mean snooty-looking?"

"That I-can-buy-and-sell-you look. And I've got royal blood besides." She laughed. She was cheering up.

21

"Okay. I'll beat everyone out by going and hanging around his P.O. box and introducing myself when he comes for his mail."

"God you're nervy. Who would ever think of such a thing?" She looked at me admiringly, no longer troubled. It was as if I'd already landed the job. "Still, Rome, honey, I'd try to look slightly meek. Intelligent but meek. See, when you apply for a job, it isn't good to look like no one can boss you around or, worse, that you're going to boss *him* around. Also smile. Do you know that you hardly ever smile? How come?"

Oh, no reason really, I thought, just that my mother hanged herself and my father cut me off, not believing that I could be a writer, making me feel that the one person I thought loved me maybe didn't, maybe shouldn't.

"Nancy, tell me something honestly. Is there something funny about my walk?"

"Are you kidding? You've got a great walk. It's your best feature."

"But a running man wouldn't even notice a walk, good or bad, as a standing man might. Why do you think he turned to look at me?"

"That's what I've been wondering ever since you told me the story. I just can't imagine!"

"Probably men walk into lampposts all the time around you," I said sadly.

"Never."

"But you wouldn't notice since you don't look back at them."

"That's true. I could daily leave men in my path with their brains on the sidewalk and never know." She climbed into bed, saying, "Good night." Nancy was good at greetings and partings even if the separation had to do only with eyelids going down, and I appreciated it. I like the little courtesies and ceremonies.

22

"Good night, sweet dreams. I'm going to write for a while, but I'll do it at the kitchen counter so the light won't bother you."

I repaired thence with pen, paper, a pot of coffee, and scribbled happily away for several hours. This was when I was happy, when I smiled. I felt lucky too. San Francisco. Living with my best friend, doing what I most wanted to do, and all my life ahead of me. Writing away, unoppressed, living the free, soaring life of the artist. I completely forgot the horrible accident, although I awoke with a cry twice in the night, my heart hammering away like it had a house to build by morning.

In the morning it was great to stay in bed rather than scurry around pretending to go to work. My dreams of the fallen stranger were heavy in my mind, however, so I called the hospital first thing on awakening. He was still in a coma, still unclaimed. My plan of the day was to sit by his bed after I stalked the P.O. box, collared the writer, and tried for the job. I checked the phone book to see what district the stated zip code was in and, hooray, it was the Marina—no bus fare! I had exactly twenty dollars left to my name: Rome Morrison.

Nancy told me where the post office was, wished me luck, and set off for the day, looking, as usual, like a star.

I'd known Nancy since I was a little girl. She lived year-round in the village where my family summered. Her father was a lobsterman, a Finn. There was a large Finnish community and they all seemed to be natural beauties, but Nancy was outstanding. Every summer one of my brothers fell in love with her but she never gave them the time of day. Everyone thought she should go to Hollywood and make her fortune but she was interested in art. She wanted to learn about it to be a critic and a collector. So she worked in galleries in cities with good museums and she took

23

courses in art history and appreciation, first Boston, now San Francisco, with the plan of ending her stint in Manhattan before returning home probably to marry a fellow Finn, bringing her incipient art collection as a trousseau.

So we were buddies because of childhood memories but also because of our love of the arts. She'd always been the one I wanted to read my stories to, because she recognized art when she heard it or saw it and because she was in touch with her feelings and could react, not as a critic, but as a reader who wanted a story and wanted "to weep, to laugh, to love life more," as Tolstoy said, because that was his aim for his readers. He didn't want them to sit there saying, "Boy, this is really archetypal."

For my interview I got dressed in my mother's clothes. Daddy had given me her clothes and, don't ask me why, when I took off for S.F., I grabbed them all and left my own. They suited me down to the ground, which is where most of them came since my mother was taller. They were all colorless, cost the earth, and were gorgeous, good-feeling materials, but why would I want to wear a hated, hanged-person's clothes?

I put on a beige linen dress and cinched in the excess with a bone-colored belt. I accessorized away with bone-colored sandals and purse, did meekness practice in the mirror, and set off for my interview.

In front of the building, damned if m Gromy wasn't going through the head-bashing pantomime again! What was the matter with the girl? Why was she so hipped on the subject? You'd think she'd witnessed a bank robbery for all the excitement it had generated. A small crowd, among them a stunning bony-faced, dark-haired man dressed in faded jeans and a sky-blue T-shirt, was standing around watching.

Of course, when she saw me she did flip-flops of joy and couldn't wait to tell them all that I was the very walking

24

woman who caused the whole thing. I couldn't imagine that they were making any sense out of it but they were and the reason was because of a story in the morning paper, describing the incident. M Gromy had it mashed into her pocket and she drew it out to show me. There was a picture of the "victim" (did they have to call him that—putting me in a perpetrator role?) with a caption asking if anyone knew who he was. It wasn't a good picture. It needed color and open eyes.

"It almost looks like my brother," the man who was so drop-dead handsome said. "But he's gone away."

Gone away? What did that mean? Was it a euphemism for death or incarceration? I always said mother was "away" when she was locked up. I wondered if it was how Daddy described me these days: gone away. How chilling.

"Why did he turn and look at you?" a stout man asked. I eyed him coldly and he had the grace to look embarrassed. "Maybe he thought he knew you," he muttered.

"It was because she's so pretty, a matronly looking woman said. I should have been pleased but I only thought she was a fool. I probably eyed her coldly too. My meekness practice had gone out the window.

"Pretty? I doubt that," the handsome guy said. I looked at him, astonished. He grinned and his bas relief of bones turned bewitching. I laughed, mostly from surprise.

"Bad enough looking like you do, but if you walk with one leg dragging the way she showed us . . ."

I laughed again, still being surprised, I guess, since I certainly wasn't amused. Unless amusement is surprise. Maybe amusement is being humiliated.

The other people drifted off. He kept talking. Who'd have thought he'd be so chatty by the look of him? You'd expect him to brood.

"Especially if it's my brother. He doesn't look at women of any description. He'd be too embarrassed. There is no one

25

on earth who embarrasses as easily as my brother. We call him the blusher."

That must really help him with his problem, I thought, and bit my tongue not to say, although why I should spare him his own medicine I didn't know.

"That's why it couldn't be him." He gazed at the picture again. "Anyhow, if he was in town, wouldn't he have called me?"

"How the hell should I know?" I released my tongue.

"That's true." He smiled, looking fully into my face. "You'd have no way of knowing, would you?"

He made me feel I was hiding something, I, who normally hid so much, but this time wasn't.

I flushed guiltily because I felt awful about the accident and did feel to blame. Again, Mother flashed before my mind, swaying. Probably deep down I blame myself for that one too. How stupid can you get? Why not blame myself for the holes in the ozone layer while I was at it?

M Gromy was standing by, watching us talk, looking from face to face but mostly at his face since it was his mouth issuing the main sounds.

Lao-tzu says, "To a person who is born beautiful, people give a mirror. But if people did not tell him, he would not know that he was beautiful. He seems to be aware and yet unaware of it, to have heard and yet not to have heard. Thus he never loses his beauty and people admire him forever."

This man, like Nancy, seemed to have heard yet not have heard. He acted like any man on any street who looked like anybody.

As for poor m Gromy, her forehead was black and blue. I put my hand on it. "M Gromy, you've got to stop describing this accident; you're hurting yourself. Don't do it anymore. Okay?"

"Okay," she said, startling me with the English.

"Her name is Lia," he said, and walked away. We both

watched him. He had a male-warrior walk, light-footed, centered. It was an I-do-give-a-shit walk.

M Gromy had a wooden box she lugged around instead of a purse, and now she went burrowing into it and pulled out another mashed newspaper page, a Macy's ad in which he was the model. We gazed at it with the same admiration we'd bestowed on the real thing.

I set off for the P.O. box. He was walking ahead of me, apparently headed the same way. I hoped he wouldn't think I was following him. I didn't go into my skulking mode but walked boldly forward. Maybe, I thought, I just drag my leg when I skulk, like Pinocchio's nose grows when he lies.

Every street-corner turn he made was the one I was going to make. He must be going to the post office. He was.

He went to the window to make a purchase. I cruised over to the boxes, located 349, and then went over to one of those high tables the government provides for your personal business and leaned against it, waiting. Presently he went to the mailbox section, extracting the mail from the watched box.

"Excuse me," I said, going over to him.

"Did you follow me here?" he asked.

"No, I was coming here to apply for the job."

"Job?"

"Aren't you looking for an assistant?"

"No."

I was stymied. "The owner of this box number put an ad in the paper for an assistant."

"I see." He was thoughtful. Then he explained. "I was just picking up the mail as a favor."

"May I come with you?"

He pondered. "I don't think so. I think you should do what the ad said and write to the box."

"But there isn't time. I need the job right away. I want to get ahead of the other people." I noticed I was pleading,

27

sounding desperate. Was I desperate? Was I going to come up with a sob story?

He said, "I would be betraying a trust. I was asked to bring mail, not a person." He paused and suggested, "Why don't you quickly write a letter now? I'll wait while you do it."

"I have nothing to say for myself. I have no credentials at all. I simply hoped to talk my way into the job. I know I can do it. I'll be good. I'll be the best."

He looked at me with commiseration—a real I'm-sorry-for-you look which I don't think anyone ever gave me before. This made me begin to fall apart. I began to cry. I couldn't believe it. Me, the utter stoic. He put his arms around me while I sobbed on his chest. This had never happened. Crying on a complete stranger's chest, a male model's. I'd never even cried on my father's and certainly not on my mother's. Whose chest had I cried on? No one's.

I boo-hooed away, blubbering out the whole story of my father cutting me off, unable to find work in Boston, coming to San Francisco. No work. Nancy depending on me. I was doing it: sobbing and storifying simultaneously. This was a full-blown sob story. I was even bringing up the leg, saying, "And now I have this dragging leg," making myself out to be a cripple on top of it all, a handicapped person, whereas I wasn't at all sure my leg even minced! "And then the horrible accident yesterday. What if he never wakes up?"

I think this was the reason I was cracking up and behaving like a fool. The accident had me terrified, for me as well as him, and those were the facts of the matter. Everything else was extraneous.

"Well, if it's my brother, he'll never have to blush again, and that would be a relief. For him and everyone else. He blushes so badly he can't even talk. He's pretty much given

28

up talking. He's discovered he won't blush if he doesn't have to interact with anyone."

I don't know how the conversation had gone from me and my troubles right over to his brother, and so quickly. He seemed to have his brother on the brain. But it was good psychology; it got my mind off myself and my own pathetic behavior, opposite from his brother's in its blushless over-interacting.

"Poor guy," I offered, to show I was not wholly involved with myself, although I was. "But you don't seem to sympathize with him and his crippling impediment. Why?"

"I hate him," he said, giving the reason why he didn't.

At first I felt thrilled to hear someone say out loud, as I so often had done, that they hated a family member but, hearing it said, and seeing his beauty diminish with the saying of it, I was struck by how monstrous it was.

I was now out of his embrace and no longer crying. His sky-blue shirt was now cloudy with a chance of rain including one dark spot where it already had rained.

I felt refreshed, ready to take arms against a sea of troubles, as the bard said, and by opposing end them.

But before I could even try out my new positive attitude, he said, "Well, I must be off," and turned to be so.

"But wait, what about the job?"

"I can't help you. I'm sorry your life is in such a mess but I'm afraid it's your problem, not mine."

He was right. And I liked it that he hadn't been moved by my whimpering, snuffling, and mewling. I would actually feel demeaned if my sob story had panned out to my advantage. I admired his resoluteness to abide by his true errand, which was to bring his friend mail, not a person. Still, I felt abandoned. It was as if we'd slept together and then I didn't matter anymore, not even enough to ask my name, not that I'd ever slept with anyone, but here I'd told him all these personal things, sobbed on his chest, and it

29

seemed like I meant nothing to him. A one-night stand. He didn't care about me at all. There was no reason he should, but still, what a rat. He seemed to have heard yet not to have heard. Mostly he seemed not to have.

"What color hair does your brother have?" I called after him, suddenly inspired.

"Red," he said. "Bright red."

THREE

Determined to get the damn job and not disappoint Nancy, I went home and bashed out a résumé on the type-writer, a curriculum vitae—which reminded me to put down that I knew French and Latin along with English. English was my trump card. What the hell, I thought, I'll astound him with my SAT score, indicate that I edited the yearbook at my prep school, and the school magazine at my college. I won't explain that I started the magazine myself to counter the tripe in the existing one. For all I know, he might be a tripist himself.

The essence of a good résumé is pithiness and mine was gloriously curt: twenty-four words including name and ad-dress! I included a cover letter expressing my eagerness, then hoofed it back to the P.O. before proceeding on to the hospital to sit with my "victim," still comatose, still un-claimed.

He lay on his back like a statue, like those stone images you see stretched out on top of their tombs in Westminster Abbey and churches of its ilk. He was graven and stern yet innocent also, like a sleeping child, with all the attendant vulnerability. I was his only protector.

Sitting there with nothing to do (it seemed rude to read and anyhow I was too hungry to read) I forced myself to think of the tear-sopped man at the P.O. who might be this

31

man's brother—forced myself because I blushed to think of him, of my behavior with him.

I was ashamed. I hoped with all my heart I'd never see him again—although another part of me wanted nothing more than to write him a long letter explaining how out of character my behavior was, how unprecedented the emotional outburst. But such letters only dig one deeper into the initial hole and appear to perpetuate the bad action one's trying to explain away. Why should he believe me anyway? I'd need witnesses to attest to my stoical nature down through the years and think of the expense, flying them all to the West Coast. An alternative would be to have someone in Boston take depositions. But Nancy, who knew me best, was here already. Perhaps she would plead on my behalf. Plead for what?

I imagined Nancy standing up to plead for me. The scenario I imagined was a sort of trial, the charge: hysteria in a government building with a secondary charge of ruining a man's shirt. Everyone in the courtroom was terribly taken with Nancy and forgot about me entirely. It ended with Nancy and the male model going off together and me being given thirty days and taken away by the prison matron with one leg pitifully dragging behind.

Which made me wonder if my dragging leg was actually some sort of hysteria-induced paralysis. I'd read of such things. It's probably typical of stoical natures that any hysteria would go to the leg.

Then I thought about how I hadn't told the model that the fallen stranger had red hair and could be his brother. Why? Well, because he said he hated his brother. I couldn't put a completely helpless man into the power of his enemy. I was responsible for him as long as he was unconscious. It was my duty to keep him from harm.

It was troubling to realize that if indeed he was the model's brother, ergo from a far place ("gone away"), then

32

no one in San Francisco would be missing him. Only when he was due back home and didn't return would someone become anxious about him and make inquiries. No telling how long that would be. I envisioned endless days at bedside. But I would be staunch.

The blusher, I thought. How painful to be crippled by one's own blood flow. He would feel about everything the way I felt about my sob-story demonstration—the kind of shame that makes you want to disappear but that colors you so brightly you expose yourself more, becoming a beacon.

The model wouldn't be an easy older brother. There was a cruelty to his joking tone.

Why did he hate him?

I thought of his arms around me. He truly had held and comforted me, a stranger. I should not forget that kindness.

An old jazz tune leapt to mind: "You're beautiful, baby, but you're going to die someday. Oh, you're beautiful, baby, but you're going to die someday. So how 'bout a little lovin' before you pass away." It was like Marvell's poem "To a Coy Mistress." "The grave's a fine and private place / But none I think do there embrace."

Donning my imaginary satin gown and cleavage, I sang to myself and the waxen blusher, who did not get up and boogie. He stirred not.

After my hospital stint, instead of returning to the apartment, I found myself buying a half pint of rum at the gigantic Marina Safeway, a coliseum of a market. My family were habitués of little markets that deliver to one's door and bill one at the end of the month. This store, as big as two football fields, ablaze with yellow light and a million packages throwing color tantrums, disoriented me. It was a long time before I found the rum bottle, the limes, the ice, and from the deli section, a plastic cup—a long time before I got to pay for these items standing in what was laughingly called the express line.

I crossed over to the Marina Green, bearing my booty, and sat on the stone wall by the harbormaster's office cutting up lime with my Swiss army knife which I always carried in my purse. I filled the cup to the brim with ice, poured the rum, squeezed half a lime, stirred it with my fingertip until it was glacier cold, and drank it. Ah, the jolt of the first sip, the facial grimace, the head hair standing up in wild applause.

I poured and squeezed another, drank it, poured a third and last. Falling into the sipping mode, I watched the sun set beyond the entrance to the bay as it had yea these many years, so naming it the Golden Gate.

Yes mother, I'm watching the goddamn sunset. Sitting here, it's impossible not to. And, okay, I like it. It's nice. Maybe there is something to sunsets after all, to sun coloring huge bodies of water and the even huger sky—a sky bigger than the Marina Safeway—almost. But so what, it isn't a poem. It doesn't make you think.

There were clouds like edifices. No, not as big as buildings, big as whole cities! Brasilia leapt to mind, since that was an architected city from scratch. I wonder whatever happened to Brasilia. Maybe sunsets do make you think, at least make you wonder what happened to certain South American cities.

It came to me for the first time that sunsets made my mother feel happy. Maybe that's why she perpetually called us all out on the porch, not for us to see the sunset so much, but to see her being happy—being relaxed, smiling, magnanimous.

I feel happy now myself, I thought. Not enough to smile but enough to charitably share the colored sky with anyone else around.

I sat until the color faded, the mountain and headlands

grew dark against the pale sky, the bridge lights came on, and a splattering of stars did too, turned on low, as they are above cities, looking dim and specklike, a travesty of a night sky. I sat a while longer, my mind empty now, what a relief.

I stood, my butt sore from the stone wall, then dumped my trash: lime skins, ice, bottle, and cup, in a nearby container before heading home to green mansions.

At the fountain, m Gromy was waiting for me, looking perturbed.

"M Gromy, what's the matter?"

She threw herself into my arms, laying her head on my breast, sobbing her heart out. "There there. It's all right. Poor old m Gromy. It will pass, whatever it is."

"Ul-ul," she said. Her version of boo-hoo, I presumed.

"Really, it will pass. I know. I was crying earlier today, and now I'm as happy as a lark."

Suddenly I froze. Was this another pantomime on m Gromy's part? Had she witnessed my humiliating post office breakdown and wished to show me she was on the qui vive, not missing any of my neighborhood adventures? If so, she was acting only the one part tonight, me—and I was being he, he who had held and comforted. Although he hadn't once said "there there," come to think of it, but instead had run on about his brother and then heartlessly walked away, not giving me the job. It was good m Gromy reminded me of his heartlessness, as I had begun to romanticize his fleeting kindness.

In case her upheaval was sincere, I gave her a kiss and a ceremonious farewell before sauntering on into the Alhambra, up the marble stairs—to Apt. 4, second floor back and green.

The next morning was Saturday. In the *Chronicle*, the column belonging to the local wit had picked up the item about the guy walking into a lamppost because of looking at a pretty girl, and added the inside information that the girl wasn't pretty, along with some twisted comment about how that should please the feminists and affirmative action. Ha, ha, I forgot to laugh, as we used to say when we were kids, if we ever were.

I'd gone out to get the paper and some croissants while Nancy made the coffee. Upon my return she excitedly told me my future employer had called asking if I would mind coming for an interview today, even though it was Saturday. Nancy told him I'd be there and set the time for two P.M. He confided to her that I was the only one who'd begun my letter Dear Sir or Madam, and that impressed him. That along with my SAT score. "What was it?" Nancy asked me.

"Perfect."

"God you're a brain. No wonder it's breaking your father's heart you dropped out. What a waste."

"Nancy, for you of all people not to understand. Who needs degrees? Degrees are for thermometers."

"You could be a professor!"

"Why be a teacher when instead I could be the one they teach about. I don't just have brains. Anyone can have brains. I've got talent. I'm an original creative person. I'm one in a million."

"But how do you *know*?"

"I don't know but I've got to find out. I'll give myself twenty years. I should know by then." I laughed. It was all so idiotic, really, writing stuff on paper. Words. What was the big deal? Why did it seem such a holy pilgrimage? It was just a craft, like Chaucer said. Like pipefitting.

"Of course," Nancy wrong-headedly encouraged, "you could give yourself just a couple of years, then, if it didn't work out, go back to college. A lot of people do that."

"I'd rather die."

At one I left green mansions and walked through Fort

Mason to Aquatic Park, where I hopped the Hyde Street cable car up Russian Hill, a rise that made Boston's Beacon Hill look like a knoll.

Over the top and a little way down the other side was a brown shingle cottage with the right numbers on it. I jumped off and, while the cable car rumbled away, having ten minutes to kill, I scoped out the neighborhood.

There was a Chinese laundry across the street. A market, ice cream shop, butcher, and drugstore were on the four corners of the cross street. I was standing in a stiff wind that hadn't existed at sea level in the Marina district. The little cottage, looking like it had got stranded on its way to the country, had red geraniums and blue lobelia in window boxes.

A tall, thin dark-haired woman with white skin and black, haunted eyes opened the door for me. She was around forty-five years old and disintegratingly gorgeous. "I'm Rome Morrison. I'm here for an interview with Mr. Wade DeRosa."

"He's on the telephone, but please come in." She smiled charmingly and gestured for me to enter. "I'm Mrs. Milton DeRosa."

Poor woman didn't have a name of her own. No wonder she was haunted.

Despite the cozy outside look of the cottage, the inside was brutally high tech: predominantly black and white with some of that red shade that looks meaner than black. Red works only on flowers, berries, and lips.

The little hallway opened to the living room from which I could see the dining-room-turned-office-against-its-will and, beyond it, the kitchen. There were probably bedrooms on the other side.

Mrs. DeRosa sat down on the black couch and picked up a coffee cup from the black table which appeared to be made of melted-down and remolded cast-iron fry pans. The furniture upholstery was so severe it looked like giant gun holsters. I felt like I was in an armory. The lamps were equally austere with crowns of thorns instead of shades. The one picture wasn't bad, however, of a cow, Holstein naturally, since a Guernsey would be fawn-colored instead of black and white. It cheered me to consider that inside the cow's mouth was a pink, soft, steamy tongue.

Mrs. D seemed to feel about her coffee cup the way I did about the room. She was looking at it tormentedly. She appealed to me. "Do you think there's a chip on the rim of this cup?"

I came over and looked at the cup, declared, "No, it seems to be okay."

"Are you sure?"

"Yes . . ." I hate being asked if I'm sure. What does it mean really? How can anyone be sure of anything for sure? But my eyes were damned keen and I didn't see a chip on the cup's rim.

"What about right there?" She pointed with a beautifully manicured nail. Her hands were long and thin and diamond rings slid around on the fingers.

I peered. "Possibly a slight discoloration on the china," I declared. "Not a chip. Uh, is this a cup a prize item, one you're especially fond of?"

"No, it's new. That's why it should be perfectly all right. My son always gives me brand-new cups so I won't worry. But I still worry." She sighed. "I so much want my coffee but, if there's broken china in it, I just can't drink it. You can die, you know, from ground glass. It's more effective than poison. And undetectable."

"But even if there were a chip in it, a chip smaller than we can see, surely it wouldn't do the job?"

"But there are so many chips off things—accumulating. There is broken glass everywhere, getting in our food and drink. Dishwashers . . ." She looked terrified at the idea of

38

dishwashers, whether she was thinking of human ones or of machines I couldn't say. The woman had a big problem.

She put the cup down. "Now you've convinced me there's a piece of broken china in my coffee even though we can't see it." She said it with an intensity that could in itself break glass.

I sat there feeling guilty, then found a solution. I lit up, saying, "Let me pour you another cup."

She shuddered. "No, no, I've probably already swallowed it. It's inside me with all the others."

On such brief acquaintance, I didn't want to get into bowel movements and suggest that she probably passed the china chips each day, that they didn't collect until there were sufficient to cut her organs to shreds. Anyhow, that would be admitting that she had swallowed them to begin with. I could see it was a trap.

Maybe she was right. Maybe we all swallowed heaps of glass splinters and china shards daily. Look at all the chipped glasses and cups in our own homes! Not to mention broken ones. I myself broke a glass or two a week. I was pretty sure the pieces went into the trash, not my stomach, but I could be wrong. If she asked me was I sure, I'd have to say—

Luckily our awkward, even tragic silence which we were sustaining while still bent over the killer cup was relieved by the entry of Mr. Wade DeRosa, son of Milton and Mrs. Milton.

"Oh God," he said, looking at me. "It's you."

It was him, the male model.

"This cup—" she began.

"Mother," he interrupted with a sort of strained calm, "I don't want to hear about it. I've called a taxi. Why don't you stand outside and wait for it. The fresh air will do you good."

And the wind will blow her away, I thought, or worse,

blow broken glass into her mouth. I knew she was thinking of the same thing because her eyes were widening with terror before turning to him with such an air of injury, I was amazed he could withstand it. The man was tough. I think he would have cracked, but just then the taxi driver came to the door.

Muffling herself, scarf over her nose and mouth, Mrs. D went away into the glass storm.

So he had lied to me about getting mail for a friend. Strangely, I was always shocked when other people lied.

Upon his mother's departure he began to glare at me. Probably he was waiting for me to burst into tears.

"I want to say at the outset that my outburst yesterday was totally out of character." I paused, stricken that I'd said *outset,* and *outburst,* and *out* in the same sentence. Three outs. End of inning—or of ups anyhow.

"I don't want to work with someone so emotional," he said flat out.

"But I'm not at all. That was an unprecedented—"

"And I don't want someone young, a girl, who's going to fall in love with me. Your name, Rome. I thought it was a man's name."

I assured him, practically pledged, "I'm not going to fall in love. I promise. I've other things to do." Big plans, beginning with eating.

"I already feel we're involved."

I did too. But what are such feelings worth? Nothing when you want a job. "Just give me a chance." I said this meekly. Nancy would be proud.

He looked me over in this new light of my meekness.

"What's your project?" I asked him. "Tell me about it. Please."

This was a brilliant stroke on my part. He stopped looking at me and turned to light a cigar, which immediately endeared him to me. Although my eye lit on it wistfully, I didn't ask if I could wear the paper ring because I was still engaged to Daddy.

The smoke raised his spirits ("A woman is only a woman, but a good cigar is a smoke") so, after swearing me to total secrecy, with a dire look that I met unwaveringly, Wade DeRosa consented to tell me about his project, which was not a book but a play. I was impressed. Here was a real contender, going up against the titan, Shakespeare, in the arena he owns. Nobody owns the novel. There's latitude.

"Here's the story in a nutshell. Take notes." He passed me a pad and pen. I seized it and almost began writing before he spoke, so eager was I for the job.

"Two brothers, a good one and a bad one. The good one is truthful, decent, fair, and just. It causes him pain to be otherwise or even to see others be otherwise. The bad brother is a trickster, a misbehaver, a troublemaker. He is the older brother, a half brother actually. Same mother, different fathers.

"He is jealous of his good little brother and grows to hate him but, despite this, his little brother loves and admires him with all his heart."

I was scribbling away and completely fascinated but spoke rather crabbily, saying, "Can we name these brothers?" I thought it was good to sound crabby so he wouldn't think I was falling in love with him, so he'd know I was all business.

"Dark and light," he named them, seeming pleased with my attitude, and continued. "Meanwhile, the second husband, who is a pretty good guy, adopts Dark. He appears to love him as much as his own son but he doesn't and Dark knows he doesn't. Dark is a bad guy and getting worse: thrown out of schools, in trouble with the law, getting nice girls pregnant, and of course making his little brother's life hell on earth."

"What about the mother? What's she like?"

"She's beautiful, and mad as a hatter. She's an obsessive compulsive. An obsessive compulsive doesn't just obsess about certain things, she is compelled to ask questions about them interminably. She asks and asks and you answer and answer but nothing you say can reassure her. Finally you want to scream. Especially if you are the bad son, you want to scream at her or, better yet, throttle her. You want to say, 'Yes, you're right, Mother, the fucking cup is full of broken glass!' And then she'll look at you as if you'd driven a knife into her womb, into the very womb that bore you but, being the bad son, her look rolls right off you and you cackle and rub your hands with glee, declaring, 'There is an entire broken windowpane in that cup of coffee.' "

"This will be a very unusual play," I said gravely. "I don't believe there's ever been a play about an obsessive compulsive."

"It isn't about her," he said brusquely. "I got carried away. It's about her sons. Well, it's sort of about her because, you see, everyone wishes her dead so they could live in peace. The father wishes it because he has a mistress he loves and who in fact the sons love too, and wouldn't it be wonderful if their beloved father could live with her and be happy at last. He can't divorce the mad mother, you see, because she's so utterly helpless and dependent. Of course the mistress wants her dead too and the sons, well, they love their mother in a complicated, intense, painful way but they can at least get away from her periodically, unlike the father. But when they're home, they wish she were dead. Even the good son does, for the sake of everyone else's happiness and also because he internalizes her madness more than the rest of us."

My ears perked at the personal pronoun, but I just bent over my pad, being magnificently imperturbable.

"Light overempathizes with everyone, but especially with

her. It's a curse. He's in such pain all the time, he can't even talk. One night, they're all together at dinner, the mistress too, because she's a family friend—and life plays a big joke. The father dies, not the mother, the father!"

"Oh God!" I groaned. Of course I was relating all over the place because it could have been my family. What if Daddy had died, not Mother. What an unimaginable blow. Although it turned out her death wasn't at all as freeing as one thought it would be when one wished about it. Anyhow, "Oh God," I groaned, looking up at him, for he was all this time on his feet pacing and gesticulating as he talked and being utterly captivating, the cigar smoke wreathing and swirling about, enhancing his gestures as if it flowed from his hands. I wondered why he didn't act instead of model. His voice was as stirring as his looks. He was terribly pleased with my groan and beamed benignly upon me so that I felt my chances of getting hired were looking good. I didn't smile back, instead, pursed my lips, beetled my brow, and bent over the pad, all business.

Pleased, he continued. "Now, listen, this is the crux. The bad son, Dark, had been going to play a trick on the mother. He poured some gritty stuff in her coffee that she'd think was glass. He wanted her to freak out in earnest.

"Now," he said, fixing me with his dark eyes so that any note-taking went by the board. "Now," he repeated, slowing down his delivery, standing still and looking solemn, "suppose Light saw Dark do that, pour something in the cup? Alarmed, but hesitating because of his admiration for his older brother, he stands up to intervene. But the cups are already being passed around . . ."

By whom, I wondered.

"Light loses track of the cup that he thinks is poisoned. But he's sure it's headed for his mother. He goes over to grab her cup away, but at that moment his father keels over.

"He thinks his father got the poisoned cup by mistake."

43

This seemed shaky to me. Two big assumptions on Light's part: first that the cup is poisoned and second that Dad got it by mistake, not intentionally. Well, I remembered, everyone *wanted* the mother dead so . . . Never mind. Pay attention.

"Light doesn't say anything to Dark or to anyone. Even though he thinks Dark is a murderer, he doesn't finger him because he is too kind, loving, understanding, forgiving. Instead, he simply goes away."

Gone away!

"He disappears. So Dark doesn't even get to tell him he didn't do it, that he was just playing one of his usual little cruel, unfunny little jokes on his mother and his father happened to have a heart attack."

"What a story!" I was on the edge of my seat, involved to the hilt.

"That's just the beginning."

"It is?" I felt like I'd sat through a whole movie, when in fact the opening credits were still rolling.

"Yes." He returned to his pacing, gesticulating mode, letting the words spill out. "Dark changes. He sees himself through his brother's eyes, sees himself as a murderer and is appalled at what a monster he has become. He stops lying, cheating, deceiving, and cruelly joking, goes to work, pays off his debts, leads a good, solid, worthy life, is particularly kind to his mother.

"Light, however, still not knowing his father died a normal death, perceives himself as an accomplice in his father's murder, sees himself as vile, and ceases to be good, for he feels it is all a mockery, a show of goodness not based on his true nature. He takes to a life of crime—"

"Does he stop blushing?"

Wade DeRosa stopped dead still and turned on me a pale, cold face and jaundiced eye, a killer eye. I froze.

"I didn't say anything about blushing." His eyes bored into mine. "Not one thing about blushing."

Through frozen lips I agreed heartily, "That's true. Nothing about blushing at all." I leapt to my feet as if answering a summons from afar. I went into a mock fluster and invented a pressing appointment. Hastily, I said, "I must go at once, but I will type up the outline and return first thing Monday morning to begin work."

I was out of there before he could say me nay, before he could say he hadn't hired me.

Employed!

FOUR

I scampered down the Union Street side of Russian Hill, sorting my thoughts, reminding myself sternly that writers were inventors, that just because the mother and brother were drawn from life, it didn't mean the story was true.

But it seemed to me that it was true, that Wade was creating this play for the disappeared brother to see so as to learn at last that he and his brother were innocent of wrong-doing.

Or could it be that in real life Dark-Wade did put poison in the cup and was trying to exonerate himself?

Or what if someone else tried to kill the mother, someone other than Wade, and it passed into the throat of the beloved father by mistake but Wade and Light felt to blame?

I was overwrought. The story had made me frantic. I should stop thinking about it and also stop running. There was no reason to run pell-mell down Russian Hill as if chased.

The thing was, it was all too close to home. It made me want to call Daddy to see if he was all right.

I stumbled and slowed to a walk but my mind still hurried.

What if Wade-Dark did kill his father, and this trick on his mother was all a red herring? He says it's really about the brothers and how they switch roles. The dining-table scene is just the beginning.

"Oh God," I groaned as I had during the telling. I went into a phone booth and called Daddy. He was in Gloucester for the weekend, said his message service. I found him there. I told him I got a job and he congratulated me. I told him my victim was still in a coma but I hadn't yet seen him today, only called.

"He reacts when they prick his feet with a pin. That's good. That means the coma isn't hideously deep. And sometimes he moves and groans and murmurs. That's good. They think he'll be coming out of it soon. If it goes on a few more days, they'll have to put a tube down his throat to feed him."

Daddy made commiserating noises. He loved a good meal himself.

"Daddy, if you wish someone dead, is that almost as bad as killing them?"

"It's bad, yes, but it's not that bad."

Daddy was good about answering questions; he never waffled.

"It's normal," he said. "You can compare it to wishing you yourself were dead. You say I wish I was dead. But it's just a mood and it passes."

"Daddy, this is terrible to ask, but did you ever wish Mother would die?"

"Yes. But all husbands and wives do, periodically, wish that of each other."

"But when she killed herself, did you feel guilty?"

"I felt sad. I still do. I miss her. But I don't feel guilty. I know I failed her in many ways. I also know I did the best I could." He paused and said musingly, even rather wonderingly, "There were times when we were quite happy."

"Do you think I'm like her? Do you think I'll go crazy and have breakdowns and make everyone's life a misery?"

"No, I don't."

"I'm never going to marry anyhow. And never have kids who might wish I was dead."

"I think you're like me, not her."

"Really?"

"Only you're braver."

"Who, me?"

"Yes. Look at you. You have gone off to a strange city at the other side of the America, the wrong side, with no money, and you are making your way in the world and at the same time taking responsibility for a fallen stranger. I'm proud of you."

"Oh, thank you, thank you. So you aren't mad at me anymore about dropping out, not disappointed?"

"Yes, I am. I'm mad and disappointed. Now I have to go look at a roast in the oven."

My mouth watered. He was a great cook. That's what he was, a cook. He wrote books, had a TV show. Right now he'd be in his crisp white chef hat and white apron, his white broadcloth shirt rolled to his elbows, and there'd be about five or seven select guests watching his every move, sipping some outrageous wine.

"I'm going to call Lily today. I can't wait to see her."

"Tell her hello from me."

"I will. Good-bye, Daddy, I love you. Thanks."

He grunted something, then hung up, which was his way of saying I love you too.

Please God, don't let anything happen to Daddy ever. Let me die first.

I stood outside the phone booth, thinking about how brave I was. The vision came to me of me, myself, and I polishing off the half pint of rum last night. Was that brave?

It was fun. We brave people have to relax sometime. Maybe I should relax right now. I had a job and I'd had this great talk with Daddy. Maybe I should celebrate. No, I had to go to the hospital and also what I really had to do was borrow some money from Lily to tide me over. It wouldn't be so hard now that I had a job and could pay her back in two weeks. But maybe I'd do that tomorrow and just go to the hospital today. And drink. And write. I still had my writing to do. I hadn't written yet today. That's what I was here for after all. That was the first priority. Drinking was second. It only sometime seemed like the first.

Back at my post at Pacific Hospital, my bedpost, I gazed at the comatose blusher, he who had "gone away," having witnessed some intolerable act on his brother's part, some seeming poisoning, possibly by the very "undetectable" ground glass itself!

If indeed he was the brother.

I scanned his features. They were not at all like Wade's, but then, he was a half brother. Did he look like the mother? Impossible to tell, he being so brawny and she so like a wraith. Although he was gradually growing ghostly himself. Those fine muscles were going to atrophy pretty fast unless he got up and doing, unless he put the show on the road. Come on, big boy, enough of this coma.

Wade seemed to favor the mad mother in his darkness, slimness, and length. Maybe in her madness too for all I knew.

It occurred to me that I was presuming Wade to be Dark and my victim to be Light. For all I knew, this man out-stretched before me could be the bad brother, the trouble-some trickster, and Wade the sweetie pie. Wade's swarthi-ness did not preclude the possibility of a blush. I remembered lines of my current favorite poet, Garcia Lorca, from "The King of Harlem:" "Blood has no doors in your night. Nowhere a blush, but under the skins, blood is rag-ing."

Even if it didn't inflame your features, you could still be

suffering the blush and the feelings engendering it, shame mostly, I guessed, shame for yourself or others, shame for the world.

But can you blush for others? Aren't you still blushing for yourself, who's been embarrassed by their behavior? If so, that's not very nice. It would seem to mean you're sitting in judgment of everyone. But if I'm going to believe this script of Wade's and all the time be trying to figure out who is who and what is what, the job will be a nightmare. I have to treat it as a play, and probably a crummy one at that. I think I'd know if I were in the presence of a Chekhov, although beauty need not preclude talent, it just seems like it should, for fairness' sake.

I grew somber thinking of Lorca. I knew I'd never come near to writing a line like "Blood has no doors in your night." So what was the point of being a writer? Why try?

Well, why not? Name one thing better to do.

Lorca was another who didn't get the Nobel Prize and should have. Frost was another. Dinesen. Daddy was right, as always. I wanted to be of their wronged number. I wanted people like Daddy, if there was anyone like him in years to come, to say of me: She should've.

This was a tough aspiration. How would I know I achieved this non-prize even if I did?

Still, what a great thing to aim for—losing!

After a while I roused myself and addressed the downed blusher thus: "Why hasn't anyone claimed you? You must have been staying somewhere here in the city. You had to change into your running clothes. Someone somewhere is missing you. It's been three days! Don't you have a girlfriend? Or had you 'gone away' from her too. If you are the brother who went away, obviously you came back. Why? And why didn't you tell anyone you were coming?"

He opened his eyes. Suddenly I was flooded with a blue-green light, illuminated by the life that lives on the other

51

side of lids. The lifted lids shut down, trembled, lifted again. More color than cognizance shone forth; it was more like looking into water than into a mind and soul, but I was thrilled. I ran out to broadcast the news to the nurses and sundry doctors, and they all said great and sent me on my way so they could examine him—only one of them making a crack about wasn't I going to sing my daily torch song before I went?

Now three great things had happened: the job, the talk with Daddy, the awakening prince. I figured I should keep my streak going and appeal to Lily for the loan.

"Hello, darling. I'm so glad you called. Your father wrote me you were here and that I might expect to hear from you."

"I wanted to get a job first and I just have. I'm so glad. Can I come by? Is this a convenient time?"

"Surely. The welcome mat's out. Come on ahead."

Lily was absolutely the no-holds-barred best of women. Her husband and Daddy were boyhood friends. She'd been like a mother to me when Mother wasn't. She was always on an even keel when Mother's moods were soaring up and down like a clay pigeon. She was always there for me—the welcome mat was always out. Unfortunately, when I was fourteen, her husband died and she moved away to San Francisco. Probably it was my fault that our keeping in touch didn't surpass Christmas cards.

She greeted me with a warm hug. She was a short, curvaceous woman with brown curly hair. It was quite a lot like Daddy's brown curly hair and, come to think of it, like m Gromy's.

Her S.F. apartment was much like her Boston one had been: small, tasteful, neat as a pin, some nice family antiques, bouquets of fresh flowers. There was a little more ease and grace about it than I remembered her previous environment having. It was restrained ease, subtle, not a descent into voluptuaryhood, no hint of the opium den, only that in her Boston apartment you tended to sit up alertly and in this one you lolled back. In this one was the extra pillow, the soft light. On her coffee table along with opera programs and acceptable magazines were a racy novel and matches from some of the livelier bars and restaurants, places Nancy went.

She was in her forties now but looked the same to me. Although her hair was bright, with a contemporary cut and her makeup careful, she didn't give the impression of trying to look young, rather of an older woman who felt good about herself.

She'd been successful in business before she married, so she was smart and savvy as well as nice. She was incredibly nice. I couldn't remember ever seeing a cross look on her face. Not that she wasn't fun too, always merry at parties but without being falling-down-drunk like my mother—or like me.

After a happy greeting we settled down and I told her all about my S. F. life: the green apartment, Nancy, m Gromy. I got hung up on the lamppost drama to where I wasn't getting anywhere near relating the Wade DeRosa job coup, let alone giving voice to my ongoing yearning for a loan.

She, like Daddy, commended my action. "You did exactly the right thing." But I wasn't letting myself get swell-headed since the truth was I'd had nothing else to do being jobless and new to the city. Also, can you take credit for good work that fundamentally you enjoy? I liked my bedpost. I was getting attached to the blusher. It was a completely successful relationship. He didn't talk back and seemed to appreciate my singing. He let me look at him as much as I wanted, and when he finally lifted his lids to look at me, his glance was completely uncritical.

Meanwhile Lily, hospitable as ever, was plying me with a

Sauvignon Blanc that made my tongue sing, along with an array of grapes, berries, and cheeses. I was having a ball. I was so happy about the whole day, and now to be with Lily again after what was it—at least five years—was heaven.

And this was the woman (me) who had sobbed over her sorry lot and dragging leg in the Marina P.O. only two days ago!—an incident I'd left out of my story to Lily thus far and would continue to leave out until my dying day, which wasn't deceit at work so much as wanting to spare us both.

I always wanted Lily to be proud of me and generally just told her the good things, whereas to Mother I'd unburden my failures. She would take the guilt on herself, which would infuriate me. I wanted the credit for making a mess of things, and with it the sympathy. It would end by my trying to make her feel better for being such a bad mother that her daughter behaved like an idiot. It would end by *my* having to forgive *her*. It was crazy. I would dig in my heels and refuse to forgive her—because I felt manipulated. But she would get so upset it wasn't worth it to try to hold my ground. We're talking tears and rending of garments. So I'd forgive her, finally I would forgive her for being such a bad mother that I was an embarrassment to her and everyone else. Why then did I go to her with these tales of ignominy and defeat only to be ensnared by the sticky web of her neuroses and guilt?

I was firing up to launch into the job-interview saga, but realized that by squashing the P.O. story, I would have to leave out Wade's great opening line "Oh God, it's you," the despair in his eyes, and much of the ensuing conversation. This virtually left no story to tell, since I was sworn to secrecy re: the play.

It occurred to me I might give Lily the floor, let her say something for a while, when the doorbell rang. I heard her greeting someone and in walked a nice-looking man whom she introduced as Milton DeRosa!

Yes, it was Mrs. Milton DeRosa's husband and he was alive. The father in the play was alive in his real life! Not undetectably poisoned in the least, not even ailing. This made me extremely happy and relieved. Only then did I realize how greatly I'd feared a real-life murder story was going on behind the disguise of the script.

Lily performed introductions and I thought for sure he's the blusher's father, being a freckled redhead although faded in both the hair and skin department, and he has the same high energy, the pugilist build, even the blue-green eyes only with a fair amount of intelligence behind them rather than my "victim's" current muzziness.

Nothing if not perceptive in these matters, I saw that he and Lily were good friends. They were happy as hell to see each other, practically dancing. It was hard for him to take his eyes off her to say hello to me.

Oh please, please, Lily, don't be his mistress. A new tumult started up in me. Relieved on the dead-father score, I now developed a cri de coeur re the mistress situation.

Why couldn't she be his mistress?

I just didn't want her to be the mistress in the script, the one at the ground-glass gustatory gathering. I thought if she were involved in that way with this family, she was in big trouble, she was in deep shit. I wanted to jump between them, waving my arms, leaping about, calling "No! No!"

Instead, I figured I should make tracks. It was too much excitement for one day, and the time had come to surround myself with green walls and try to integrate a few things, primarily try to ascertain why I wasn't acquainting the DeRosa family with the facts about their comatose son and brother.

Wasn't my possessive protectorship of the boy unwarranted, unnatural, even abominable?

Still, if he was regaining consciousness, he could make these decisions for himself.

55

I exited. At the door, Lily put some bills in my hand, saying, "This is to tide you over to the first paycheck, darling. Come again soon."

What a woman.

I realized I was famished. My hunger of the past weeks, joining the inner tumult over the script, was clamoring to be assuaged now that I had cash in hand. Lily's grapes and Brie had only piqued it. What my tummy really grumbled for was bacon and scrambled eggs and English muffin with blackberry jam, hard to find in a San Francisco restaurant at five P.M. So I bought the ingredients at a corner, human-sized, market, returned home without having to run the gauntlet of m Gromy or Nancy, cooked, gorged, and slept. I was so hungry I forgot to drink.

FIVE

When I awoke at eight A.M. on Sunday, I decided to get Wade's writing out of the way so I could do my own. Nancy had spent the night elsewhere, so I could take over the dining table and make as much mess and racket as I wanted to. Having had breakfast the night before, I contented myself with fruit and coffee and set to work.

I found it was hard to write someone else's words. I naturally wanted to improve on them. The play opened with everyone at dinner. Well, where was this dinner? Who sat next to whom? What were they wearing? Was it a happy occasion to begin with? What time of year? Weather?

I certainly couldn't add this information on my own. Would it be impertinent to list these questions for Wade's perusal? He certainly would need to think about them if he was to adequately set the scene for the patricide. I wasn't upset about it now, even wondered why I'd let the story freak me out. It was just a story and the father was alive and kicking and if Lily was his mistress, so be it. It was none of my business.

I spent the rest of the day at my own writing. I didn't go to see the blusher, as I'd come to think of him, because I wanted to stay home and write and read. However, I did call the hospital. The report was that he was unchanged, which surprised me because of yesterday's breakthrough of the open eyes. Nurse Wiggin, my favorite, who would have filled me in with a lot of details, was off duty and the nurse I got was brusque. I told her I'd expected he'd be sitting up, taking nourishment, playing with blocks or doing a crossword puzzle. "Well, he isn't," she said, and I could get no more out of her.

When I arrived for work Monday morning, Wade had changed the action. "I've changed the opening scene," he announced before I'd even shrugged off the stone-colored jacket to reveal my sand-colored blouse and pants (rolled at the bottom, belted at the waist).

"Why don't you wear clothes that fit?" he asked curiously.

"They're my dead mother's."

He waited for more. When I remained mute, he said, "I like them."

"Thanks."

This time we were more professional, establishing ourselves in the office which, unlike the armory, had wood and color: blue walls, oak floor. On the teak table were computer, printer, fax and Xerox machines, phones and tape recorders—all of which I knew how to use. I was actually more skilled than I realized. Jobs turned out to be a lot like everyday life, especially if you have a world-famous father you've helped out from time to time just for fun.

Wade was wearing a white terry-cloth bathrobe that came to his knees and gaped open at the (bare) chest. Was that professional? Was it even a teeny bit conducive to a respectful working relationship? Should I ask him to get decent, or blithely ignore his semi-nudity?

I had about thirty seconds to decide what tone to take because it was the sort of thing one had to comment on at once from the outset. Establish parameters, not even wait until I'd looked my fill. It would be wise to keep on with

58

the crabby personality I'd tried out on Saturday, all business.

"Mr. DeRosa," I said, sitting down at the table and striking an efficient attitude, "before we begin, please put some clothes on."

He looked nonplussed. This he was not expecting from the new secretary. Possibly he was surprised because he forgot he was still in his bathrobe. Probably I was the first person who'd worked for him in his house and this was his normal A.M. outfit, as it was mine when I could indulge it.

His surprise was fleeting, however, for after only a beat he said, "I didn't dress because I was thinking we should make love right away and get it over with."

I blushed hotly, then began giggling like a fool. If I'd surprised him, he'd really surprised me. I'd expected him to either carp or oblige, not come from left field with an outstanding proposition. My hand had flown to my throat. Was it to start unbuttoning my shirt that it had so flown?

I'd be damned if I'd let him out-surprise me. "Good idea," I said, pushing back the wheeled chair and standing up.

Now *he* was blushing a little bit. Blood *did* have some doors in his night. Maybe his blood wasn't raging beneath his skin but it was definitely percolating. Downward, for that matter, if I was to gauge its flow by the escalating bulge beneath the loosely belted robe. This stimulating sight caused more hotness in my face, I who rarely if ever blushed. This scene was definitely getting out of hand. Time to be crabby again.

But how be crabby and be unbuttoning at the same time. My hands, as if their own creatures separate from me, with their own behavioral patterns, had gone to work. And now his hands were helping. Not only that, his penis had pushed through the gap in the robe. I eyed it eagerly—it was my first penis. I blushed away. Was this shame? Embarrassment? Who for? Or had the house furnace come on, causing me to overheat? I was certainly hotter than I'd ever been. Maybe that's why my hands were removing my clothes—to cool me off. His loosely belted robe was now unbelted. In fact, it was loose on the floor, as were my clothes.

"You're so hot," he said. "God you're hot!"

"I know." Clotheslessness was no remedy, because now, with his hot skin flush against mine, I was on fire. I began to sweat. Was this customary? Should I be embarrassed by these rivulets of water or was embarrassment itself causing this physiological flash flood? Was I ashamed? Was this love? Sex? Shouldn't we lie down pretty soon? My legs were giving out.

Now we were on a bed. What were those noises? Whose? His finger was in my vagina. It felt wonderful. More noises. His lips were on my nipples. Our bodies were sopping. But that finger. It was like a torch igniting my insides. I was turning all molten within. It felt so fabulous but almost too good to stand. Maybe I could die from this. I wanted to beg him to stop and also to keep on. Then I yelled as my body felt some release from the excruciating sweetness. Now his finger was growing huge. This would never work. But he was grasping me with both arms so it was no longer his finger, it was the robe divider.

Now *he* yelled and his body went into a spasm, roaring to life as if it had been kick-started. Then I gathered the act was completed, was gotten over with. The good idea was executed and I was no longer a virgin and I'd discovered this whole other world I never suspected from readings or tellings, that I sensed could be my undoing. Or maybe my doing. Because why would I ever want to do anything else? How did anyone do anything else once they knew about it? How did they go to work?

The bedroom was warm, colorful, cozy, and normal, with tapes scattered around the boom box, athletic gear, posters on the wall, clothes draped on chairs, a pile of paperbacks by the bed. It could have been Anyman's room, unlike the living-room decor which sought to make a statement: Your money or your life.

An hour later I resumed my seat. We'd showered and dressed and bundled the sweaty bloody semeny sheets into the washer. We'd had a good talk. I thanked him for opening wide the gate to this flabbergasting world of the senses and he tutored me on protection, giving me the name of a clinic to stop by on my way home where I could get a prescription for my method of choice.

He told me about San Francisco's plague of AIDS, which I knew, and assured me he'd had an AIDS test and even today, despite our sudden sexual onslaught and headlong rush toward consummation, he'd remembered a condom as usual. When we'd gotten this business out of the way, he gave me a starter lesson in providing extra pleasure although, he said, I was a natural, being highly passionate, and would be giving him lessons before the week was out.

Back in the office, he lit a cigar. "Now," he said, pacing about as seemed to be his wont, "in the new opening scene, no one dies." He grabbed a pocket-sized tape recorder and his voice went into its mellifluous professional mode. "The good brother, Light, *is* a blusher, as you penetratingly suspected on Saturday. In fact, the play will be called *The Blusher.*

"They are all at table . . ." He looked at my list of questions and answered them. "It is autumn. They are in a mansion on Pacific Heights in San Francisco. Rain is slashing against the huge windows. There is a fire in the fireplace. The women are gorgeously dressed and bejeweled. The father wears a tie but is casual in sport jacket and slacks. Dark wears jeans and T-shirt. Light is in a suit, an Armani. There is a young woman there too. After all, there has to be a love interest. She is dressed simply and is nothing to look at but her beauty is illusive and grows on you.

Was this me, I wondered with wild surmise and some alarm. Was I now to be included at the murder dinner, along with dearest Lily?

"It isn't clear which brother she belongs to," he continued, "and at this point I don't know who is sitting next to *whom* as you would say.

"And I don't know what the occasion is or if it's happy. Maybe everyone is just being fairly pleasant and making an effort to be polite and interesting. Although, naturally the bad brother is glowering—except when he looks at the young girl. Then he releases a rakish smile as if it were on springs."

I smiled and said, "Nice!"

He executed a small swagger and proceeded. "It is coffee time and the maid is passing the cups around. The bad brother is doing the pouring over at the sideboard. From a small packet he pours some gritty substance into his mother's special cup which has a different design from the others, and the good brother, who is the only one positioned to, sees this act. As Dark passes the cup to the maid to give to the mother, Light intercepts it. He stands up, of course, to do so, blushing furiously. He takes it, blushing the while, blushing for me, for my evil nature, and carries it away to the kitchen. He dumps it out and never knows it isn't poison. He goes away out the kitchen door into the raging storm, drenching his Armani suit. He disappears from all of their lives that very minute so Dark can't tell him it was only a joke."

He turned off the recorder. "Aren't you going to groan?"

I smiled. "This is very good. I like it."

"You can transcribe it at home if you want. I'm out of here. I have a shoot way the hell down the coast in Santa Cruz."

Can I come with you? The words clamored to be said. Can I?

"Beachwear," he elucidated. "I've made a list of things I want you to do, but as soon as you're done, take off. Your hours will be flexible. Be here at ten tomorrow."

"Okay." Greeting and parting ceremonies being so important to me, I wondered if he was going to kiss me goodbye. I sort of lifted my face a little. But he didn't. Could it be he'd made love only "to get it over with" as he'd said?

The door closed behind him and my raised chin slowly dropped to my chest.

Within two hours I'd fulfilled the chores he'd set for me. I walked home, stopping at the clinic, deciding on the pill. As I came near the Alhambra, I hoped that m Gromy the omniscient wouldn't have an erotic pantomime prepared for my delectation to show she was up on my latest activities. She was there, rummaging around in her box, and didn't even greet me. This hurt my feelings, so I stopped to inquire. Maybe she was mad at me. Maybe she felt abandoned that we were no longer fellow virgins. "Hi, m Gromy. How're you doing? I had my first day of work today with Wade DeRosa, your friend the model."

Her rummaging abated but she was giving me only half an ear and none of her eyes. "I'm helping him write a play but actually I spent most of the time on the phone about his modeling career. He's very successful. Everyone is eager to have him. They want to buy his voice as well as his looks and sometimes the two together for a TV ad." Her face was turned away so I came around to where I could see it better, and her mouth was turned down like a tragedy mask.

"What's the matter? Did you lose something from your box?"

"Mingle," she said. "Mingle nd ly." She showed me the

63

box and it was completely empty. All her treasures were gone.

"M Gromy, this is terrible! Did someone steal your treasures?"

She nodded and was suddenly energized enough to rise from her squatting position to pantomime someone walking hastily by, grabbing everything out of the box, and then going into the apartment building with it.

"Who?"

She sputtered out some irate words, pointing at me. "Me?"

She went on to make certain uncanny gestures and mannerisms that mimed Nancy.

"Wait here. I'll see about this." I stormed in, up, and back, to the plastic arboretum. I found Nancy going through m Gromy's pile of things.

"Nancy, how could you? That girl, m Gromy, is absolutely devastated that you ripped off all her treasures."

"She's the ripper-off, the little bitch. You know how the mailman leaves the magazines that can't fit in the box on the hall table? Well, she's been going through my magazines and tearing out the pages she likes. Mostly pictures of this one gorgeous guy." She waved some pages from *Vogue* and *GQ* showing Wade in all his glory. Well, most of his glory. Only I had seen it all. (I and probably hundreds of other women, I reminded myself, if he's the bad brother his play portrays him to be, deflowerer and impregnator of nice girls galore.)

"So what, Nancy? Let her have her pictures. She knows him. She adores him. He's nothing to you."

"You mean he lives around here? Boy, he sure will be something to me. Why haven't I ever seen him?"

"No, he doesn't," I said hastily. "He used to," I added, which was true and which was why he still had his P.O. box in the Marina. "Before the earthquake."

64

Why wasn't I saying he was the man I worked for to my best friend? I wondered if I was psychologically unable to tell the truth. This one was a lie of omission. I wasn't lying so much as hiding things. I was a hider. I was a protector, of myself mainly, but also of others. I was a person of extreme privacy. It was as if I were afraid my life would be taken away from me if people knew about it. And I was right. Nancy, now that she'd seen his picture, wanted to take away Wade.

I could tell m Gromy the truth about things because I sensed she knew them already, maybe even before I did, and I knew she'd never hurt me. She'd be on my side.

"That little retard bitch," Nancy exclaimed.

I was shocked. "Magazines," I said. "We're talking about magazines here. Paper!"

"I love my magazines. I pay for them. I like to have them new, in mint condition, like some people need their morning paper, clean and unread, not grubby from dirty hands and certainly not torn to pieces. Is that unreasonable?"

"You took *all* her treasures!" I gestured at the buttons and feathers and stones and shells and postcards, little windup toys and crayons. "You're the bitch. I'm surprised at your cruelty. And she's not retarded in the least. She's foreign. She's smarter than you. Maybe even than me," I added dubiously.

"Give me a break!" Nancy rolled her eyes as if I were retarded too.

I got a paper bag and put all the things in it including the pictures of Wade. Nancy grabbed one of them back and it ripped. For some reason tears sprang to my eyes. "Now look what you've done."

"Rome, what on earth is the matter with you? You're acting like a maniac."

"I don't like to see my friends abused," I yelled maniacally. "I'll buy her magazines—"

"What about buying some food for the apartment while you're at it?" Nancy yelled back.

"Here!" I threw a bunch of bills at her from the roll Lily had given me.

I stormed out and gave the paper sack to m Gromy, who embraced me with gratitude. I told her to leave Nancy's magazines alone, that I'd buy her her own. Then I went back to the apartment and apologized to Nancy, and she laid some things out to me along the lines of how to be a roommate.

"It isn't just money I want, I want help. I want you to do the marketing sometimes. I want you to cook sometimes. And I definitely want you to clean a lot of the time. I've been doing everything. I've been pulling the whole weight. I was willing to while you got on your feet. You were a mess when you arrived and my heart went out to you. You were thin as a door and you were walking around like you had a club foot. . . ."

"Why didn't you tell me?" I squealed. "I even asked you if I was walking funny and you said my walk was my best feature."

"It is your best feature. That's why I didn't say anything. I didn't want you to think the best thing you had going for you—besides your brain, of course—had gone south. Anyhow, you did it only sometimes. It was like a nervous tic. It came and went." Nancy started to laugh, remembering.

"Here I thought I was going around like a woman warrior and I was really looking like Quasimodo. Did I sort of hunch my shoulders too, with my head lolling around my waist? No wonder that poor guy walked into a lamppost." Now I started to laugh. We laughed together until the tears came. What a day this had been! Life was really something. It didn't stop for a minute.

"But where did you get the money?" Nancy asked. "Advance on pay?"

"No, from Lily. She lives here. Remember Lily?"

"No."

"You don't? The one who was like a mother to me?"

"Nobody was."

"She'd come to Gloucester for weekends with her husband. A really nice woman. Pretty."

"So many people came weekends, it was always a huge party. You'd stay at my house."

"You'll remember her when you see her. Maybe it wasn't that she was like a mother, it was I wished she were. One time I came upon her and Daddy cooking together, chopping up stuff, and at the same time they were singing in close harmony."

"You can bet if they were married, the singing would stop pretty quick and she'd be doing the cooking alone while he was kept late at the office or, in your dad's case, kept late at the Boston Wine and Food Society dinner."

"What a cynic. And you're the one from the happy family. Maybe that's why you don't have to fantasize."

I don't have to fantasize anymore, I thought, because I'm happy at last. I have a job, a lover, three friends. I'm on my own . . . writing. . . .

I was lying.

But why wasn't I happy?

Because he didn't kiss me good-bye.

Pitiful.

SIX

After supper, which I penitently bought, shopped for, and cooked, I went to see my downed blusher, who I expected would surely have gone from the tremblingly lifted-eyelids phase to bright-eyed and conversational, since it was now day five. But no. He was pale, still, out like a light. "Put a twenty-dollar gold piece on my watch chain and say that I died standing pat"—a line from St. James Infirmary sprang to mind, then to lips and voice.

"We think you must have imagined it about his eyes opening," Nurse Wiggin said, a bushy-haired, hatchet-jawed, sweet-eyed woman. "He's the same as ever. If anything, a bit worse." She withdrew, popping her head back in to add, "Sorry to interrupt your song."

My heart plunged. I sat staring at his stony features. "Come back," I said. "I feel like you're clinging to this coma. Life is good out here. There's fun to be had. There's sex!"

I looked around. We were alone in the double room and presently no one was in the next bed. The door was ajar but mostly closed. I was thinking I'd have a look at his penis. Now that I'd seen one, I felt curious about others. Quietly, softly, I folded back the sheet. His hospital nightshirt was scrunched up so his genitals were exposed. I was stunned by the fiery mass of his pubic hair, far brighter than the hair on

69

his head and in tight kinky curls. His testicles were rosy pink, especially against the almost green paleness of the rest of his skin and they had a rough, hidelike look, like elephant skin, but if anything were softer than the rest of him. His penis was thicker than Wade's, just as his all-over body was more chunky and muscular, and it was very soft. I knew because I was stroking it. It looked so sweet and vulnerable. Hard to believe how the organ could change from a flimsy rag to a thruster with the power of ten. In no time at all, if Wade's was any example. But my victim's poor one lay on his inner thigh like a discarded toy.

I was enjoying the moment. Combined with my morning memories, I began to feel mildly aroused. Wait! Was it stirring just a little—a fine tremble like yesterday's lifting of the lids? A flutterment like a baby bird ruffling its feathers? It gave a little flop as if trying to rise from the nest where thigh met groin. I looked at his face. It seemed to have some expression, not lively but definitely less mask-like. I continued my ministrations. I put my mouth to his penis in the way Wade had instructed me, licking and sucking and sort of swirling it about. Now it was coming alive and growing by leaps and bounds. I was getting lost in the operation and, realizing this lack of alertness on my part was perhaps unwise, I unloosed my mouth to look at the patient, who orgasmed away—fountaining from one end, groaning from the other, his eyes wide open and rolling in his head.

I was not alone to see this definite sign of improvement, for the wall seemed positively lined with staff, white on white, save for the red faces. Talk about blushing. Talk about life not stopping for a minute but wishing it would so I could get out of there.

"Where the heck am I?" the blusher asked. Or the non-blusher, in this case, since he was the only one in the room who wasn't red-faced. Looking mystified, he sat up wob-blingly.

"Just what is your relationship with this man?" the doctor asked me. "I thought you didn't know him, that you were strangers."

"I'm his girlfriend," I said just as my victim flat-out denied my statement by asking, "Who are you?"

"You're in the hospital," I reassured him. "You've been in a coma." I paused, then added meaningfully, "You've forgotten everything." He flat-out denied this statement too, because when the doctor asked him his name he said "Rusty DeRosa" right off the bat.

Then he smiled and said, "I just had the most wonderful dream."

Everyone looked at me. I shrugged and looked humble.

He lay back and closed his eyes. "I think I'll have a little nap." He opened his eyes and said, "Hospital?"

"Yes," said the doctor. "You've been in a coma for five days. I'll explain. But first, is there anyone you'd like us to notify? We haven't known your name until now."

"No, please. Please don't tell my family I'm here."

"See," I said. "I knew he wanted to lay low."

"Who are you?" he asked again.

"She's been very concerned," Nurse Wiggin said loyally. "She's sat by your bed for hours every day, talking to you, even singing to you and"—she beamed—"now this!" She waved extravagantly, even proudly. "She kissed you awake. She's your girlfriend. You probably have some amnesia. You may not remember some of the time leading up to the accident."

"Accident? Girlfriend? Singing to me?"

I shrugged again, humbly. I hoped it wasn't going to turn into a nervous tic like my dragging leg.

I went home. I was pretty tired. I figured I could use a little nap myself. It had been a big day: new job, losing my

71

virginity, fight with Nancy, kissing a coma victim awake. I doubted I would ever have a bigger day than this. I guess this was what it meant to be a writer, living to the hilt. Too bad it made me too tired to do any writing.

I got up early the next morning to transcribe Wade's tape of the opening scene. As I made the coffee, I played the tape to refresh my memory.

With Lily's money I had blown myself to some French Roast, and the smell alone made me feel raring to go. The worst thing about being poor had been drinking Maxwell House—worse even than not drinking rum. Well, I did drink some rum when I was poor, but not enough. Was it being poor and sober that made me drag my leg? Or was it leaving home? Was it Daddy cutting me off and not believing in me? Was it postponed grief and guilt over Mother's suicide death?

I paused as Wade's voice on the tape penetrated my thoughts, saying, "It isn't clear which brother she belongs to."

I decided not to think about it. I had, at the outset, sworn off relating this infernal dinner party to real life. Anyhow, Milton DeRosa was alive. And the blusher who had gone away was now returned—to San Francisco and to consciousness. So forget it. I'm just a secretary doing her job. Secretaries often bed down with their bosses. . . .

And do they often kiss their boss's brother's penis? On the same day? When the boss's brother is unconscious and can't participate . . . can't even express willingness? Isn't this rape? You could be up for rape. God knows there were enough witnesses.

There I was, back in the courtroom: "Your honor, it was my second penis. I got carried away. Also I thought it would do him good." A lie. Add on a charge of perjury.

"Your honor, m Gromy will vouch for my charity, morality, forbearance, and vigor, which are four of the six perfections in Buddhism."

"Speak," says the judge.

"Mingle nd ly," says m Gromy.

All eyes are on Nancy as she comes next to the stand and is sworn in. "She is definitely vigorous." Nancy damns me with faint praise, citing only the fourth perfection. "Except when it comes to cleaning and shopping." She begins a long lament about what a crummy roommate I am. There's not a dry eye in the courtroom. . . .

Enough, enough. To the typewriter. Transcribing time.

"They are all at table," said Wade's voice. "It is autumn. . . ."

Nancy came into the kitchen with the morning paper, which was being delivered now that we were economically sound. "He's awake!" she screeched. "And he's a . . . a scion, whatever that is, the heir to the Rose Department Store. Listen: 'The mystery man who turned to look at a woman who wasn't pretty and ran into a lamppost, knocking himself out, has been lying unclaimed and unknown in Pacific Hospital . . .' "

"Nancy, I know he's awake and I've got to type this up before I go to work."

"But did you know he's from practically the most prominent family in the city?"

"All I know is he didn't want them to know. Someone finked. Probably the doctor, who's a heel. Now, do you want me to keep this job or not?"

"I'm sorry I read aloud about the unpretty woman. . . ."

"Forget it. The reporter naturally has to milk it for all it's worth."

"At the end of the article they say, 'Now maybe the more pressing mystery will be solved—why he turned.' "

We both laughed.

* * *

When I got to the Hyde Street cottage and Wade let me in the door, I was dismayed to find him out of his robe and dressed for the day. "Mother's on her way," he muttered, not kissing me hello, "Here she is now."

A taxi door slammed and she was high-heeling it up the wooden steps and into the door ahead of me, almost through me. She began talking to Wade as if already in mid-conversation. "You know your father takes only *The New York Times* and *The Wall Street Journal*." She flung off her wraps. (It wasn't a coat or a jacket nor yet a shawl. I didn't know what it or they were) and lit a cigarette, dragging deeply the venomous smoke. This woman, who was afraid of imaginary glass getting in her system, was sucking in certified poison for all she was worth!

"So I didn't see this picture in the *Chronicle* until Cook showed it to me last night. I think it's Rusty"—she pulled out the picture Wade had already seen—"except that he'd never in a million years walk into a lamppost because of looking at a pretty girl, and this girl apparently wasn't even pretty. What do you think, Wade?"

"I've seen it. It does look like Rusty, but it couldn't be him."

Obviously they'd neither of them seen this morning's paper. I looked around the armory where the three of us were standing. Yes, there Wade's newspaper was, still rolled up in its elastic band.

"This is the girl, by the way." He gestured at me as if I were not the girl but the lamppost. "Rome Morrison, who you met the other day and is now my secretary."

"This is what girl?"

"The lamppost girl."

"Really? But I think she's quite pretty."

"She is when she blushes."

"Everyone is prettier when they blush. I think we should all be red instead of white or brown. Also, blushing is so touching. Except in poor Rusty's case, where it is a disfigurement. I myself haven't blushed for years."

"You don't have to; we all blush for you," Wade said.

"Ha!" She laughed in a perfunctory way as if to acknowledge she knew he was joking, but she personally didn't see the humor. Of course he wasn't joking. It was one of his surprising remarks that sounded like a joke but wasn't. Neither of them, I realized sadly, had any humor.

The two were intent on each other. "I think people look pretty when they laugh," I offered, just to show I was there in the room with them, with a tongue of my own, but they shook their perfect heads and said in unison, "Wrinkles." Then Mrs. D said, "Anyhow, Wade, I want us to go to the hospital together and look at him and be sure. The taxi's waiting."

"It's a waste of time."

"I insist." She stubbed out her cigarette and rewrapped herself, her nervous hands arranging and rearranging the garment. I eyed it keenly. Was it a cloak, a toga? She rose to her feet and peered at the table. "I think I burned it. Did I burn it?" she asked me.

"What? The table? The table's okay."

"Is my cigarette out?" She peered into the ashtray.

Peering, "Yes."

"Come on, Mom." Wade from the door.

Three times she came back to look at the ashtray and the table. I realized it wasn't only that she was compelled to do this, it was that she couldn't trust her own senses. She really couldn't see that the cigarette was out or that the table wasn't burnt. If she could take it a step further and tell herself there wasn't a table there anyhow, she'd be okay, or even better, tell herself that she wasn't there, that none of us are here.

Wade called to her fretfully, "I haven't got all day to do this. We go now or never." She made me promise to keep an eye on the stubbed cigarette. I promised but I could tell she didn't trust me. I sat down and fixed my eye on the butt. She wrenched herself away convinced that the cottage would burn to the ground in her absence, sending me a last lamenting glance to grapple me to the table.

It worked. I sat there looking at the cigarette much in the way I had sat looking at Rusty when he was in a coma. My bedpost had become an ashtraypost.

I didn't want to think about what would happen when they found Rusty at the hospital. I felt confused by Wade's behavior toward me, or his lack of behavior.

I was still in the chair when Wade returned twenty minutes later. He sat down on the couch and looked at me.

I looked back at him, beginning to smile, then thinking better of it as he said, "You know, you're a colorless person, but yesterday when I said, just for a joke, let's go to bed and get it over with, you blushed and were suddenly nice-looking. Your skin colored, your eyes sparkled, and then you laughed, showing these beautiful teeth which in turn illuminated the curves of your lips and a never-suspected dimple hollowed your cheek. You threw back your head and there was this gorgeous long neck. Fuck, I thought. And fuck I did."

"Yes . . ." I wondered where this was leading.

"Today you look colorless again. My mother was just being nice saying you were quite pretty."

"I know. She was just buttering me up so I'd watch her cigarette stub." I laughed, forgetting it would make wrinkles. Think of being colorless *and* wrinkled. My smile faded as my hurt feelings began to take charge.

I knew sex was bound to have a down side, and this was it, getting easily hurt by the person you had sex with because he tells you you're not pretty, which you already knew. Which everybody knew. After all, it was in the papers two times.

76

"He checked out."

"Oh?" I almost screamed. Then I realized Wade didn't mean Rusty died, only left the hospital.

"Yes. The receptionist said *Mr. DeRosa* checked out."

So he knew my victim was his brother. Now what?

"What's your game, Rome Morrison?"

"Croquet."

He scowled.

"D'you play?"

"Shut up and listen. My brother comes to town and nobody knows he's here. Because of you, one way or another, he's knocked unconscious. *You* pay his bill at the hospital. You, who supposedly had no money and had to beg me for a job. You, who followed me to the post office and threw yourself at me. You knew he was my brother and didn't tell me. You kept it a secret."

I remained quiet. This was not a court and he was not Your Honor. The hell with him. If he'd buttered me up like his mother had, maybe I'd squeal. But he did the opposite, unbuttered me, scraped me. You don't sit down and tell a person they're colorless and then expect them to explain all their actions of the last week. Especially when you haven't kissed them good-bye or hello after becoming lovers, after becoming one person together.

I could tell he was genuinely angry with me and honored the fact, wrongheaded though I thought it was. But I wasn't disturbed by his anger. The great thing about growing up with four older brothers, loving them, and loving your father too, is that men don't scare you one bit. They can be mean and hurt with words or fists, but you learn to hold your head up and look them in the eye and not be daunted, not cry.

"The only thing that makes sense is that you knew Rusty before and you're here to spy on me."

"Spy on you and learn what for whom?"

He was stymied.

I figured I deserved asking a question myself, so I picked the most burning one. "Where has your brother been?"

Wade didn't answer my question any more than I had answered his. So I picked the second most burning. "Why did he leave? I really so much want to know your family story. I want to understand about you and Rusty." He was silent and I tried another one. "Why do you think he came back?"

Wade threw himself full-length on the couch and flung an arm over his face. "I don't feel like working today," he said as if suddenly losing interest in Rusty. "Let's go to bed."

"I don't want to go to bed with you. I hate you."

It was true. I'd arrived all on fire to make love with him, but now I felt cold cold. Not just because he said I was colorless or accused me of spying or ignored me when his mother was here, but because I didn't like him. He was a cold, possibly mean person. He wasn't at all like Daddy except for the cigars. The cigars threw me off. He had no kindness, wisdom, or humor. He was a rat.

I saw him looking at me from under his arm. Then he was levitating, up from the couch, on his feet, across the floor, pulling me out of the chair into his embrace. Instantly, all rancor fled. I wanted to make love to him more than anything in the world.

But while my body was giving in, my mind, not so quick on the backpedal, was kicking up a fuss.

Thoughts, struggling to be heard over the roar of physiological sensations, reminded me that I had just told myself and him I hated him. And I meant it. Does my body have more say than my mind? Just because I want to have sex again with all my heart, am I going to capitulate?

If so, if my mind loses, then I also lose my mind.

This could be how Mother began to go crazy.

This is another down side to sex, going crazy. I need my mind to write with.

I wrenched away from him much as his mother, earlier, had wrenched herself away from the illusionary flaming table.

"No!" I said. "I quit."

I headed out, tucking in my shirt, grabbing my jacket.

"What about me?" he cried. "What about my play?"

I strode down the gigantic Hyde Street hill, my quadriceps reminding me of the previous run down the Union Street hill the day I got the job and was so happy. Now look what I'd done.

I fetched up in Aquatic Park, a small beach flanked by long piers and breakwaters with a maritime museum hunkered behind it. I stood in the icy water, then I sat down in the sand, my head in my hands. Behind me some sports began beating on bongo and conga drums, sounding like machine-gun fire on the wrong speed.

I could be lying in his arms right now.

I could still have a job and the promise of money to live on, not to mention paying back Lily.

I was back where I was, only worse, because I owed Lily and because I didn't have the blusher to go and sit with when there was nothing else to do.

And what would Nancy say? Talk about tragic looks. The others would be only warmups for the look I'd get tonight.

I won't tell her. I'll pretend I'm still working.

I was back in my deceit. With spades.

But never mind. I'd stayed pure in heart and true to myself. I didn't leave college and come out here to hold a job. I came to write. And if in any way I defiled myself, it was defiling my writing. If my mind told me the man was a rat, I had to listen to it and not let my body push it around with its fanatical desire for the man or for the sex experience. It was hard to separate the two, and maybe you couldn't. I certainly had never craved the experience with anyone else. There was something about his touch that set me off, threw switches all over my body. . . .

I moaned. Just thinking about him made me hot. I took my head out of my hands and looked around carefully to see if anyone heard me moan.

I saw the most amazing sight. About ten old men were going into the water, very old men, with brown, gnarled bodies. They were going into the frigid water and starting to swim away. What did it mean? Was this a euthanasia program?

I jumped to my feet. "Save them! Save them!"

"Take it easy, honey," said a large woman sitting on the step behind me. "It's just the Dolphin Club swimmers. They do this every day, year in, year out."

Internally, I changed my cry to Save me! Save me!

There was no one even to go to, to pour out my troubles to. I wished Mother were alive.

Mother, I've done it again. Made a mess. A complete mess. Yes, you're right. It's all your fault. It's because you're such a terrible mother, so crazy, selfish, self-absorbed, un-available, unloving. No, I don't forgive you. I don't. A million years can go by and I never will. All right! All right! I forgive you!

And Daddy had been so proud of me for getting this job, coming out here all on my own and finding work. No, no, wait! He said he was proud of me for taking care of the fallen stranger. That was it. I'm sure that's why he was most proud of me. Maybe it was both. He said I was brave. Didn't he say I was brave? I think he did. I must continue to be brave. And be proud of myself for quitting this job with the rat.

Would Daddy be proud of me for the way I woke up the stranger? I think he would. Yes, Daddy's different. He doesn't judge the way Your Honor does, and all the others. He understands unusual measures. He's a chef. Chefs try things. He would laugh and be pleased.

Thinking of Daddy, I cheered up. After all, I still had a hundred of Lily's money. And there were other jobs. And I really didn't like working on the play. It got me upset. And he had behaved badly to me, calling me colorless the very next day. And I was a writer. That was the most important thing. That was my true identity. I was not a scorned lover, a limited roommate, an orphan by suicide and by Daddy not supporting me, which, why should he? He was right. I still think he was right. I see his side.

But I'm right too. To do what I want and have to do. Even if I fail. I'm right to try. It will be a life well lived.

SEVEN

When I got home, I was amazed—also perturbed but mainly amazed because it was so out of context—to see Mrs. D standing by the fountain with m Gromy. While the seal calmly balanced water on his nose, the two of them talked animatedly, executing flamboyant gestures, m Gromy's arms going like windmills. Mrs. D's body language was only comparatively more subtle, her arms moving as if they were doing a two-handed wall painting on a bumpy wall with deep cracks in it. As her gestures waxed, m Gromy's waned until her arms hung listlessly. Occasionally, she shrugged but pretty soon gave that up too. Her head hung down. She looked sullen and defeated. Seeing me approach, Mrs. D flung herself toward me, capes and shawls flying. "I must talk with you."

I bypassed her to give my buddy an encouraging hug after her verbal, or at least gestural, beating. She clung to me for a moment, then, inspirited, took up her box and shambled off. Although m Gromy had gotten the worst of it, I had to hand it to her that she had managed to *engage* Mrs. D in a conversation. I myself had never gotten more out of her than neurotic questions. M Gromy definitely had power. I turned to Mrs. D, who said, "You're all sandy."

"I was on the beach," I said needlessly. I sat down on the tiled bench. The seal was spouting the water three feet in the air and a light breeze was fanning it out as it fell, catching a rainbow in its watery net.

"I left you at Wade's." She sat down beside me.

"Nothing burned," I assured her. "I stayed until his return, my eyes pinned on the ashtray. When he got home, I quit the job. I'm not working for him anymore."

"Oh no!" she wailed, a thin, piteous cry. "It's my fault." She wrung her hands together. "Please don't quit. He needs you."

"It's not your fault in the least. It's his. He made me mad." Called me colorless, I thought. It began to seem funny.

"He was upset about Rusty," she defended him. "That you hadn't told him. Of course we none of us believe that story of his turning to look at you."

"It was in the papers."

"So are a lot of things," she said dryly. Somehow I hadn't imagined a dry tone in her intense tonal repertoire.

"M Gromy saw it happen." I felt like I was back talking to Your Honor and putting forward m Gromy as a witness.

"That isn't her name. She just says it a lot. Her name is Lia. I wish she would stop hanging around here. We used to live here in the Marina before the earthquake." She gestured around at all the pastel buildings. "Our house collapsed and we moved up the hill. She just can't seem to adjust to her new neighborhood and returns here every day like a homing pigeon."

"Is she your daughter?" I was flabbergasted. This family seemed put together at random.

"Of course. I thought you knew that. I thought she introduced you to Wade."

I realized that she sort of had.

"I'm very nettled with her that she didn't tell us Rusty was back," Mrs. D went on. "She saw the accident, it turns out, but never said a word to us that it was Rusty. Not that she has words."

Here was my chance. "Why did Rusty go away?" I asked breathlessly, still wanting to get at the heart of the family drama.

"Because of him beating up that reporter and practically leaving him for dead. It was a scandal. And here we are, a prominent family. Although you wouldn't know it to look at us, Lord knows. To look at us up close, that is, as you have done. Luckily, prominence is not in the eye of the beholder."

I was badly shaken. Rusty? Did this mean he was the bad brother? Did this mean that fair is foul and foul is fair, as the Macbeth witches always insisted? All this was happening too fast for me now. I couldn't integrate so much news. What about the dinner party? Where did that come in? Was the reporter at the dinner party?

"Anyhow," she continued, "please don't quit on Wade. He needs a nice girl like you. You are the best thing that has happened to him."

Niceness wasn't in the eye of the beholder either, if she thought I was nice. I looked at her admiringly. She was enjoying herself. She seemed to thrive in the open air. Mentally ill people should be made to stay outdoors, where things couldn't get to them. Maybe that's why Mother felt good watching sunsets. Because they were outdoors. All her hysterical fits, deep depressions, maniacal rages, and suicide attempts were indoors. They never happened while she was watching the sunset. I felt I'd made an incredible breakthrough in mental health, something Freud or Jung never considered, being indoors all the time themselves—since that's where sex, dreams, and bowel movements all take place.

"Wade was upset by discovering Rusty was here and was injured." She continued her motherly defense. "And of course he's always upset with me. He probably took it out on you. Forgive him. Forgive us all. Please come back to Wade."

I loved it that she was so open and pleading. It was irresistible. "All right, I will."

Why not forgive him? What was there to forgive, really? So he'd called me colorless. Big deal. I *was* colorless. Most people didn't see me at all, let alone in monochrome. He was calling a spade a spade. And I was being a sorehead. Also, any brother of m Gromy couldn't be all bad. Except maybe Rusty.

"I must go now. Thank you for being so understanding." She rose from the bench in an easy motion, started off, and then turned. She was the master of this sort of thing. Her son's dramatic potential was only a shadow of hers. She asked, "What will you do about your sand?"

"Wipe it off, I guess."

"Be sure it doesn't get on anything."

"I will." I knew what she meant. Be sure it didn't get into her coffee cups.

Raiment fluttering, she strode away. I watched her go. She had a fine, strong, rapid walk but was not a good navigator.

In my apartment I let the color green wash over me, seep into me. "Green, green, how I love you, green." Another line from Lorca. And, similarly, "Green, green, the riverside grass," from the great Chinese poet. I say *the* great because I believe all the wonderful Chinese poets were really one man who lived for a thousand years: fishing the rivers, climbing lofty peaks, saying farewell to friends, going off on long journeys, and taking care of the emperor's business.

The green did me good. Better than had the blue of Aquatic Park. When I awoke it was twilight and the buzzer beckoned. No good asking who was there through the intercom because whoever it was always sounded like a cow mooing.

When I opened the door, there stood Rusty. It was fine to see him on his feet. It was fine to see him. I felt myself light up. Then I remembered that he'd beaten a man nearly to death. It probably wasn't true. I had the feeling Wade and his mother lied almost constantly.

"Come in. You look pretty good. How do you feel?"

"A little shaky." He looked tentative. He sat down on the edge of the green Naugahyde armchair, ran a hand through his red curls, smiled shyly. "Thank you for looking after me. I brought a check to repay you." He placed it on the coffee table as if it would be coarse to have money pass hands between us.

"Thank you, Rusty."

"Did you really sing to me?"

"Yes."

"I can't believe it. Nobody's ever sung to me. I'm . . . so touched."

"It was fun. I've always wanted to sing to someone." I laughed, feeling happy and appreciated.

"Would you sing to me again. Now?"

"Well . . . I guess I could. Maybe you should lie down, though, so I can pretend you're unconscious and won't feel embarrassed."

Obligingly, he lay down on the green-covered bed, mine. Hands behind his head, he closed his eyes. I sang "Cocktails for Two." "In some secluded rendezvous, that overlooks the avenue, with someone sharing a delightful chat—of this and that, and cocktails for two. . . ."

He opened his eyes and smiled at me with dumb pleasure. He looked utterly happy. One of his hands dropped over his cock, which made me wonder. I blushed. Maybe he was called the blusher because he made other people blush. The song sort of dried up in my throat. He opened his arms and dumbly, with a dumb, happy look of my own, I went over and lay down beside him.

He put his arms around me tenderly. "Nurse Wiggin said you were my girlfriend."

"Uh . . . yes, I . . ." Now I again remembered he'd beaten a man to a pulp. I wanted to ask if it was true but didn't want to destroy our tender mood.

These brothers were really something. So was I. I was completely up for having a (consenting) sex act with Rusty, which was odd since, earlier, my fine noble writer's mind had forbidden what my body yearned for with Wade, who hadn't done violence to anyone. Except for maybe trying to kill his mother or father, I reminded myself, and it sort of took me off the hook and made Rusty the good brother again. Since he'd only bashed someone almost to death, he was an acceptable sex object. Embracing him would not compromise the bullshit artist within me.

But nothing happened. We just sort of fell into each other's eyes, letting the dumb, happy look stream back and forth between us. He said, "I still don't remember the time before the accident. I don't remember why I came back to San Francisco. I must have met you recently."

"Well . . ."

I heard Nancy's key in the lock. My impulse was to jump up, but it seemed rude to Rusty. It would be behaving as if I weren't really his girlfriend, which I wasn't, but he didn't know that. So I didn't jump up but decorously rearranged myself and he did what men do to settle down their cocks.

Nancy was pretty surprised to see me alongside this stranger. We stood up and I introduced them. He said, "I can't remember if we've met," which no man ever could have said to Nancy before. I quickly explained about his memory loss so she wouldn't be hurt.

"That gorgeous model is outside," Nancy said, rather flustered.

Rusty and I looked at each other not-dumbly. Both our eyes seemed to be asking if there was a back way out. It was an avenue I hadn't explored even during my skulking days.

Just then Wade appeared at the still-open door. I couldn't help but feel it was a good thing he hadn't walked in with Nancy and seen me and Rusty sprawled together looking into each other's eyes for all we were worth as if we were trying to exchange corneas.

The brothers hugged each other. They wrapped their arms around and held on. It wasn't brusque. It had feeling and warmth. Right then I gave up once and for all trying to figure the family out. It was incredible how the play had thrown me off, how I had *believed* it so thoroughly that it had clouded my perceptions and judgment.

"Are you okay?" Wade asked him.

"Except for some temporary memory loss."

"Lucky you. I'd give my eyeteeth for some memory loss." He looked at me as if I'd be the first thing he'd like to forget.

"I'm not quitting after all," I said, remembering my promise to Mrs. D. He looked majestically unconcerned at the news, which probably meant he was pleased.

I introduced Wade to Nancy, explaining that he was "Rusty's brother and my boss." She gave me a look telling me what a devious bitch I was to have kept this from her about Wade being my boss.

A silence fell and, feeling strained, I wondered what would happen next. It was easy. The brothers left, both saying, almost in unison, that they would see me tomorrow.

Nancy looked at me accusingly. "What on earth have you been doing? I'd forgotten this about you. I'd forgotten that around you, people's lives end up like a ball of yarn the kitten's been at."

"Really?"

"Yes, really. And it's because you go your own way. You

don't tell people things. It's not that you connive and manipulate. You don't. And you don't have a malicious bone in your body. But things get all balled up anyway. I wouldn't be at all surprised if you are fucking both those brothers and haven't even admitted it to yourself because it's such completely unacceptable behavior. At the same time, I have to say I admire you. And I have to say I'm jealous. God, what's he like?"

"Which one?" I asked. And we both broke up laughing.

EIGHT

I didn't see either brother the next day. At work there was a note from Wade saying he'd gone to L.A. for three days to film a commercial. He left instructions for holding the fort and a new tape to transcribe of the script. This I decided to put off doing until the last day so I wouldn't get confused and upset again.

After work I met Lily for dinner at a restaurant in North Beach, the city's Italian section fast falling to the Asians. I had fettuccini with a motherload of garlic and downed a lot of harsh red wine. My ears were perked like a puppy's as I listened to Lily tell me about the DeRosas, which I'd asked her to do.

Along with my usual nondescript, ill-fitting, dead mother's clothes, I wore a suede jacket Daddy gave me when I turned eighteen. The suede was the color my hair would be if it had color. It did illumine my eyes, made them look tan instead of dishwater.

Lily was in lilac silk and looked like an orchid. I always felt proud to be in public with her and pretended she was my mother. I like to think she pretended I was her daughter, but I could never ask her just as I couldn't ask her if she was having an affair with Mr. Milton DeRosa if my life depended on it even though it was on the tip of my tongue to do so. With my real mother I could ask anything under the sun. Maybe it's because if you hate someone, there's nothing in the relationship to protect and you don't have to be careful of their feelings.

Anyhow, I figured while she was telling me about the DeRosas, her situation vis-à-vis them might emerge. I wondered if she realized what a volatile family it was and that if she was his mistress she could be in danger. Maybe all mistresses know they're in danger; it goes with the territory.

Now that I knew about sex, I could see it was worth risking your life for, and it was wonderful to think it had the same power over old people. Wade himself was an older man—probably in his late twenties.

"Milton owns and runs the Rose Department Store, which, in this city, is right up there with Macy's," Lily said. "He's a member of the Pacific Union Club and the Bohemian Club."

I remembered that sort of thing had always impressed her. Position in society mattered. I forgave her. I think I did. I found myself wondering if she'd have jumped for joy so much seeing Mr. D the other day if he was the same guy only the janitor. But that's too easy because the same guy wouldn't be the janitor. Would he? No, he'd have a different psychological makeup as well as a different tailor.

The thing is that my mother was from a great Boston Brahmin family arriving just a few ships after the *Mayflower*. She fell in love with my dad, who was just some kid frying her a hamburger at the other side of the counter. Of course she was out to infuriate her family too. That was her m.o. all her life, to infuriate everyone, so maybe I can't give her credit, but that was one thing I always gave her credit for: true love regardless of the guy's background. She didn't know he was going to be a world-famous chef.

She was happy with him, gave him four sons, took a procreative break for five years, then gave him me and went crazy. After I was born she began to lose her beauty and her wits. She couldn't handle Daddy's fame. She thought every other woman was after him, and they were. Women are crazy about him. They all feel about him like I do. He's nothing to look at, but he's so wonderful.

I tuned in again to Lily, who had come to the end of Mr. D's boring accomplishments. "His wife was married before to (she named a dead actor) and Wade is his son. Rusty and Lia are Milton's and hers. Lia is special. They've taken her to every specialist and tried every teaching technique, but it's hopeless. She can't, or won't, speak English."

She was talking about m Gromy.

I became mildly agitated. "Specialist! Specialist! There's nothing wrong with Lia that having a different mother wouldn't fix. Good God, Lily, when you see someone as tough as Wade fall all to pieces around her, clench his jaw and grit his teeth, imagine how it would be for a young girl, a sensitive young girl? Nor has Rusty had an easy time of it. Boy, I wouldn't speak either if it meant having to answer neurotic questions the whole time. Lia was smart enough to figure out a way to save herself. She went one better—made up her own inscrutable language. Easier than blushing so bad you can't speak, or gritting your jaw so hard you can't!"

Lily laughed lightly. "Take it easy, darling. You're projecting. You're talking about you and your mother."

"I suppose I'm *special* too," I said bitterly.

"Yes, you're very special."

"Well, I got partly educated and I'm making it on my own." (By borrowing her money, I remembered.)

"Yes, you are and I'm very proud of you, but you did get thrown out of three schools and it is too bad that when you astounded us all by getting into college because of your college boards, that you didn't *stay* in."

"I had more important things to do." (Discover sex.)

"I'm behind you all the way," she said equably. "How about some dessert?"

"I'll have a cappuccino. Lily, is it true that Rusty beat up a reporter?"

"There was a rumor to that effect," she said vaguely as she waved at the waiter. She gave the coffee order, then said, "The man never pressed charges."

"Why did Rusty leave town, then?"

"I don't know. Milton never talks about it. You'll have to ask Rusty."

"What's the deal with you and Milton?" I asked, thinking the hell with it. What's she going to do if she doesn't like the question, call the police? Ask for her money back? Tell me to mind my own fucking business?

"I love him with all my heart," she said.

"It is a filthy, wet, and bitterly cold evening in November and people will be arriving for the dinner party, shedding their coats and hats and scarves, folding up their umbrellas, feeling exhilarated because San Franciscans love rain, feel grateful for it, even reverent. You'd think they were all farmers counting on rain for their livelihood."

So Wade began the latest version of his play, which was now being called *The Dinner Party* rather than *The Blusher*. I was lounging on my bed, holding the little recorder in one hand, a cold rum in the other, believing that in this comfortable position I would feel less anxiety. I knew Wade was going to spring something awful on me. The possibilities were endless.

"The mistress is the first to arrive, looking exquisite, not a hair out of place from the wind and rain. She is let in by the teenage daughter of the household, who does not respond to her cheerful greeting but walks away. In the background the wife can be heard screaming inarticulately at the

94

husband. The mistress remains expressionless. The husband appears, looking wretched."

MISTRESS: *(exiting)* I'll go to her.

HUSBAND: Good. You're always the best at calming her down.

The doorbell rings and Dark arrives with a young girl.

DARK: *(to his father)* This is my fiancée.

The girl blushes but the father doesn't react because Dark introduces every girl he brings to the house as his fiancée since it's easier than remembering their names.

DARK: I suppose that's Mother screaming.

HUSBAND: Lila has just gone to her.

DARK: *(to fiancée)* Lila is my father's mistress but she pretends to be the family friend. My mother believes she is her friend, her own special best friend. She doesn't know Lila is doing everything in her power to take her husband away from her.

HUSBAND: *(to fiancée)* Please don't believe anything he says. I don't. For instance, you're not really his fiancée, are you?

DARK: *(turning to the girl)* Will you marry me?

FIANCÉE: *(blushing)* Do you suppose I could have a drink?

They walk into the living room and she stands by the bar while Husband fixes their drinks.

The daughter is huddling by the fire on her haunches and remains there the entire time, stony-faced, endlessly patient, like an aborigine watching his mastodon meat being cooked, not realizing it could cook by itself, that the fire was browning it, not the gaze issuing from her hot, stony eyes.

Meanwhile Lila, the ersatz family friend, is dressing Wife and trying to soothe her. Scene is in Wife's bedroom (presumably Husband's too).

WIFE: He is so cold, Lila. He is ice, ice. He's warm and sweet to others but to me he is arctic ice. He hasn't said he loves me for a year. He never takes me in his arms, never a kiss. Oh, sometimes he'll possess me in the night, half asleep, not knowing what he's doing, but never a caress, never a kiss. It's killing me. I'm shriveling inside. My skin is like autumn leaves, sere, all juice and color gone. I crackle to the touch. When I move, I hear my bones grind.

LILA: Come on now, darling. Look, here is one of your prettiest dresses. *(Slips it over her head)* There. I'll brush your hair. It is still so beautiful.

WIFE: Still? Did you say still?

LILA: *(laughs lightly)* Compared to mine, I mean. I color mine. And it's so thin compared to yours.

WIFE: Oh, Lila, you're so good to me. Sometimes I think you're the only one who loves me. I know the children don't. They wish I were dead. So does he.

LILA: Nonsense. Come on now. You look lovely. Let's go and meet Wade's fiancée.

WIFE: *(laughs)* Another one?

Both exit laughing. And the wife, laughing, does look lovely. She is far, far more beautiful than the mistress, more beautiful than the beautiful young fiancée standing by the fire with her drink. The wife and mother is heartbreakingly beautiful and everyone in the house, except the young fiancée, hates her, especially her special friend.

Silence. I turned off the tape. "Oh God," I groaned. "Oh God, God, God. I feel sick." I sat up, put down my drink, put my head in my hands. "I knew it. I knew I shouldn't listen. I knew I should stop working for him. He's such a rat. Such a horrible, horrible rat. Oh, Lily, what are you doing with this family? What am I doing? And I have been promoted now to fiancée, when originally I wasn't there. Then I was only barely there. Now I'm practically a main character. And he portrays Lily as a villainess of the deepest dye, and it's not true, not true at all. He's so mean. What is he doing? What is the point of this play? Does he know I'm Lily's friend?"

Suddenly I was distracted as my glance fell on the coffee table and didn't see something, the check for three thousand dollars which Rusty had put there two nights before. It was gone. Either Nancy had put it somewhere, Rusty had taken it back, or Wade had stolen it.

Gleefully, I eyed the void. It cheered me enormously. My nausea subsided. It was so much better than thinking about *The Dinner Party* and it meant I couldn't transcribe the tape because a disappeared three Gs couldn't go uninvestigated. This was a major priority. I called Nancy at her workplace and she said she had noticed it on the table when she arrived the evening she met Rusty, but not again since.

That brought the investigation to an end pretty quick since Wade was still in L.A. and I didn't have a number for Rusty. Still, Lia might know something. She always did.

I poured another drink and carried it downstairs and out to the fountain, where I found Lia and Rusty sitting together on the tile bench, not talking, watching the fountain as if it were a TV, looking peaceful.

"I was just coming to see you," he said, rising to greet me. Despite it being mid-morning, neither of them look surprised at the patently alcoholic drink in my hand. Rusty sat back down and I sat at the base of the fountain, facing them. Like a magician, m Gromy reached into her box and came up with the check, saying, "m Gromy." She added, "Rankus muckle indly droit. Bwa nruda m Gromy lint."

"I gave her the check to keep for you, but she either forgot about it or didn't see you yesterday," Rusty explained. He regained his place on the bench, then added, "I didn't want Wade to see my address on it. I didn't want him to know our private business either."

It was a foggy morning but warm. The air seemed muffled. It was hard to believe we were in a city. The splashing water could be a nearby brook. We could be sitting in a wood.

97

"He already found out I paid for your hospital bill," I said. "He thinks I'm a spy for you because of the coincidence of my taking a job with him."

He laughed. "Wade thinks everyone's a spy because he's such a snooper himself. You know the old saying about the man who looks behind a door is a man who has stood behind one."

I looked down at the check and saw that Rusty's current address was in Chicago. He'd gone away pretty far although not as far as I had.

Lia wandered across the street to the Marina Green, where a man was flying an enormous, highly complicated kite. In no time she had the string in her hand and, not understanding the principle, began running in zigzags all around the green as if teaching the kite to play football. She even had one arm held stiffly out before her to ward off any tackling kites. It made me smile.

"I'm a writer," I began to tell Rusty about myself. "I'm nineteen. My home's in Boston but I sort of ran away. Did you run away?"

"I'm twenty-one, too old to run away. I got away. From my family. It seemed like a good idea. It was an even better idea to come back and get knocked out by the lamppost because I don't blush anymore and I can talk. It's wonderful. It's a miracle. Apparently, I turned to look at a pretty girl and crashed into the thing."

"No. She wasn't pretty. She was me. I'm really not your girlfriend." I told him the whole story, all but the dick-sucking part, but maybe he knew because he said, smiling, "Nurse Wiggin told me you woke me with a kiss."

I shrugged. "Well, yes, I guess I did."

He got up and came over to me. It was only a few steps. He reached down and pulled me to my feet. "I owe you my life. . . ."

I wanted to shrug again, but he had both hands on my

shoulders. He was looking at me with immense sincerity. I glanced down to the fountain base to see if my drink was okay.

"I owe you my ability to talk. Rome, I want you to be my girlfriend because I love you."

This was silly. He couldn't love me when he didn't even know me. Still, I was moved. Moved almost to tears. No one had ever told me he or she loved me.

The same words leapt to my tongue to return to him because it seemed to me that I loved him too, beginning with when he was unconscious, more when I saw his aquarium eyes gleaming from his weakly fluttering lids, more again when I kissed his cock. I adored him when, on my green bed, he held me close in his arms and gaze. But I couldn't say so yet. There was the matter of the man he attacked and abandoned. I decided to outright ask him as Lily had suggested.

I sat down on the bench and looked up at him. "Rusty, before we go ahead with this, I have to know about the man you apparently beat up. Is it true?"

"Yes," he admitted, and with the admission he looked mighty pleased with himself. "I knocked him to the ground," he said with relish. He actually did a little boxer's dance step while he told me this, his arms up in the classic position.

I was dismayed. "Had he injured you in some way?"

"Not at all."

"Well, I'm sorry," I said dolefully, "I can't love a vicious bully."

"Wait. Let me try to explain. You see, I was always such a good guy. Everyone always thought I was so great, everyone who knew me, that is, which was already too many. Then, when the earthquake came and the Marina was hit, I saved some people. I'd go into the collapsed buildings to see if

99

anyone was hurt and couldn't get out. It looked heroic but it wasn't anything.

"This reporter found out about it and was going to do a story about me, so I knocked him to the ground. What else could I do? I didn't want some stupid story making it seem I was something special. Also it felt great to hit him, to do something bad for once. It was a huge relief. I didn't fracture his skull or anything. It was nothing like what you and the lamppost did to me. There were medics all around."

"You sure were bad." I smiled.

He didn't smile back, still being serious and dead sincere. "Well, it helps that everyone thinks I did something bad and I'm rid of that burden of being so good. You'll find me much easier to love now that I'm normal and can talk besides."

"What about Wade? Is he a good person?"

"I love Wade," he said stoutly. "I thought it would help him too if I went away, because we were always being compared."

"Rusty, have you remembered why you came back?"

He smiled happily. "I guess I had a date with a lamppost."

"Why do you think you turned to look at me?"

"Because you're so beautiful."

"You big liar!"

He laughed, delighted to be called a liar to add to his bad streak.

I began to feel sexy and thought how to widen the streak even more. There's nothing like a man telling you you're beautiful and that he loves you to make you feel desire for him and when on top of that you've had two rums . . . "How much did Nurse Wiggin tell you about the kiss I gave you?"

"Not much." He looked completely open to the idea of being told more about it.

"Uh . . . do you want to come up to the apartment?"

He jumped up and put out his hand in case I needed helping up from the bench. I did, but it was that happy gaze from his crystalline eyes that pulled me up, up, and into his eager arms.

We made love, and not only was it fun but it made transcribing the tape virtually impossible.

Rusty was a virgin. I told him I almost was in that I had made love only one time before. I didn't say how recently (three days ago) or with whom (his brother). He was feeling too happy and so was I.

Perhaps it wasn't as knockdown, dragout exciting as it had been with Wade but ten times more loving, sweet and fun. We talked a lot and were playful. He didn't get up and turn into a boss right before my eyes who wouldn't even kiss me good-bye when he left and would start calling me colorless first thing the next morning after ignoring me in front of his mother and not kissing me hello.

But never mind all that about Wade. I didn't even think of him the whole time I was with Rusty because it was so nice.

Maybe this *was* love. Maybe it was. It sure seemed like it might be.

He was easy to be with. I had the same good feeling with him that I had being with Daddy, only better, because he was my own age, didn't care that I'd dropped out of college, and perceived me as a writer.

Along about five we got dressed because Nancy might be coming home. I rustled us up a little supper of stir-fry shrimp and vegetables over brown rice and he ran out for a bottle of wine. When we sat down he said, "I can't imagine someone making love to you only one time. Who was it and how long ago?"

101

I frowned and looked my most menacing. "It is very bad of you to interrogate me."

Of course he lit up at my calling him bad.

"Rome, will you marry me?"

He reached his hand across the table, and I wanted to take it, but I said, "You are getting carried away. Eat your supper."

"Of course I'm carried away. Who wouldn't be?" He paused and said gently, winsomely, "Rome, I do love you. I'll take care of you. You can write day and night. . . ."

"I just never did plan to marry, Rusty."

"Be flexible. Change your plans." His hand was still stretched out and his eyes were streaming away at me again with their tourmaline light.

"I shouldn't have children. Craziness skips generations. You shouldn't either. Although in our cases, maybe it didn't skip."

"Okay, no kids. Anything you want or don't want."

"What do *you* want?"

"To make you happy."

"To *be,* I mean. Rusty, put your hand down." He was still holding it out to me. In the air. His arm must be starting to hurt. He laid it down on the table, palm open, for me to take when I was ready.

"A fireman." He smiled a little sheepishly. "Then I can save people, only it will just be my job. Also I get to wear a uniform and drive a big shiny red truck with a siren. I'm strong so I've passed the physical test in the top ten. Now that I can talk, I'm not worried about the orals. A blushing fireman would have been pathetic and ridiculous. So, will you please marry me."

"Maybe," I said tentatively, "we could be secretly engaged and see how it goes."

"I want to tell the world."

"Well, you can't. I never tell the world anything. I don't

102

tell even Nancy. Although," I considered, "I may want to tell Daddy."

"I'll want to tell my dad too, and I want you to meet him."

"I have met him."

"Impossible. He never goes to Wade's. I'm afraid he doesn't care much for Wade who, you might not know this, is his stepson."

"Yes."

"The fact is, Dad never goes anywhere except to the store or his clubs because he always feels he should be looking after Mom and Lia."

He looked at me questioningly as if to say, so how could you have met him?

I couldn't bring myself to say that I met him at Lily's.

Who was I protecting by not saying it: Lily, Milton, Rusty? Why must I, right off the bat, in this brand-new important relationship, adopt my old stance of deceit?

"I guess I didn't meet him," I said feebly.

Rusty took my hand and put it in his open one that was still lying waiting on the table for my consent.

NINE

Before bed I called Daddy, who was in Madrid. I was able to reach him, waking him up.

"Hi, Daddy, it's Rome."

He grumbled and made me hold on while he went to the bathroom. Then he came back on the line, asking, "How is your victim?"

"He's up and about and wants to marry me."

"He shouldn't be held responsible for anything he says until he's completely well."

I laughed. "Better me than Nurse Wiggin. His name is Rusty DeRosa. He's twenty-one and going to be a fireman in Chicago."

"Do you love him?"

"Yes, I believe I do. But, Daddy, it seems too easy. I never expected to be happy and to live a normal life. I don't know if it will be good for my writing."

"It will be very good for your writing. It is hooey about having to suffer. Coleridge says you do your best creative work when you have 'a quiet conscience, a condition free from anxiety, and above all a healthy digestion.' I have certainly found this to be true for my cooking—especially the last."

"I have the last but not the first two."

"It's hard to be free from anxiety, but a quiet conscience

is up to you. Your character is up to you. If it is bad, you must never blame anyone although you will be tempted to blame your mother. You must especially not blame me."

"You'll like Rusty."

"A father is always suspicious of a man who sleeps with his daughter."

"He paid me back for the hospital and I put the check in the mail to you."

"A likely story."

"You are in a silly mood tonight."

"I feel pretty good. I had a wonderful dinner at Horscher's. Actually, this is the first day I have felt pretty good since your mother's death. Rome, one thing Coleridge left out. Love. I did my best creative work in those first ten years with your mother. I will never again be the great chef I was then. Your mother was the love of my life. I wish you could have known her then. When I remember her, I remember how she was then."

He fell silent. I waited for more but there was no more. That was a lot. I had a huge lump in my throat and he probably did too. "Thank you, Daddy. I needed to hear that. It gives me courage somehow. Good-bye. Love!"

"Good-bye, Rome."

I resolved not to go to sleep right away. There was much to reflect upon like: maybe love and marriage were good creatively only for men. So I got into bed and lay on my back with my eyes open and stayed that way, thinking deeply for almost a minute. Then I relinquished myself to the big free-fall into sleep—that weird other world we go to every day of our lives.

The next morning in Wade's office I distastefully transcribed the tape accusing Lily of villainy. He was due back from L.A. that afternoon. I typed up a list of his twenty-three phone messages, five of them from women, the rest business, not including the eight, count them, *eight,* from his mother, who called constantly even *knowing* he was away. I didn't like to think how often she called when he was home, although maybe when he was home she just spent the day here. It apparently did her good to hear his voice on the machine and to pour out her worries and anxieties onto the tape or onto me if she got me instead of the machine. I began to see that she must make his life hell on earth.

My mother didn't attach herself to her kids. The opposite. She sent us all to camp and boarding schools so she wouldn't have to see us and, if we were home, choose that time to travel.

She didn't want to inflict herself on us. Unlike Mrs. D, who was an inflictor par excellence. What a relief it must have been to Rusty to get away. He thought it was the lamppost stopped him blushing, but I was sure it was the time away, maybe both. I wondered what could help Lia.

I took my bag lunch over to a little tucked-away Russian Hill park and maybe I fell asleep on the bench (another tiled one) because it was mid-afternoon when I let myself back into Wade's cottage. He was there. On the telephone. Speaking to someone about me.

"I think Rusty was in love with Rome, followed her to San Francisco, was looking for her all over, saw her by chance, and, wheeling to look and be sure, crashed into the lamppost. That would explain his turning to look—and his connection with her since."

"I'm here!" I announced myself.

"I know," Wade said to me, glancing my way. He said good-bye to whoever it was, surely Mrs. D, and asked me, "Am I right?"

"No. But maybe he was looking for a particular girl and he thought I was her. He still can't remember."

He wore a beautiful tan suit, white shirt, flowered tie,

107

and seemed to be in a good mood. His hair was a helmet of raven feathers.

"Maybe he'd never met you but you were his dream woman, his perfect fantasy, and when you passed, he thought, that's her!"

"What a lovely explanation," I said, smiling.

"You're such a romantic. It's pitiful."

"I guess I am."

"Whereas I like sex for sex's sake." He looked at me with his smoldering eyes, purposely intensifying the natural smolder.

I felt aroused. I did. The man had incredible magnetism. My arousal was subtle. I made no display this time. There was no redness, no rivulets of sweat (that he could see anyhow). I didn't rip off my clothes. I locked my hands together to keep them from my buttons. And from shaking.

"Did you see your messages?" I asked in my crabby business voice.

He ignored my question. Instead, asked, "What did you think of *The Dinner Party?*"

Swallowing my feelings, I detached myself enough to honestly say, "I thought it was good. Dramatic. Suspenseful. I think it's a good idea to have the entire play turn around the dinner party. The dialogue's great. You really can write."

"One of the questions you first asked about it was: Were they celebrating anything?"

"Yes?"

"I've decided it should be an engagement party."

I froze.

"I'll title it *The Engagement Party.* Not only will it ostensibly be to celebrate their son's engagement, but everyone there will engage at some time during the evening and then, *of course,* there will be an engagement with Death."

"Of course," I said dryly, sort of a croak.

He remained staring at me, smoldering away. "Why did you decide to come back to work for me?"

"I needed the money," I said coolly.

"Sure," he said.

"Look, Wade, you said we had to make love just to get it over with. So we did. Let's just leave it that way."

"I suppose we could leave it that way. It's just that I like to be the one to decide."

"Okay, fine. Consider it your decision. A good one too."

"What's the deal with you and Rusty?"

He phrased the question in the very way I had put it to Lily regarding her and Milton, but I didn't answer as she had: I love him with all my heart. As soon as I didn't, I wished I had. I felt disloyal to Rusty. But Rusty had said he didn't want Wade knowing our private business. Also, did I love him that much? It was still so soon.

I tried to speak forthrightly and be square. I said, "When Rusty was in the hospital, I didn't know for sure he was your brother, but I thought he could be. I didn't tell you because he was my victim and I felt it was incumbent upon me to protect him."

"From me?"

"Yes. Because the day you saw his picture and said he looked like your brother, you told me you hated him. Now that I've seen you together, it doesn't seem to be true."

"Never mind my feelings about him. What are yours?"

"I like him a lot."

"Everyone does. He's incredibly likable. And I'm not. It's always griped me. If he weren't my brother, I suppose it wouldn't matter. You'd think it would be enough that I got all the looks and the brains. But it's not. I want to be nice too. I want to be perfect."

He shrugged, then swiveled the subject and the mood which, briefly, had been one of quite amazing honesty and

109

intimacy. "Fuck it! Who cares? But if you quit on me one more time, that's it."

I almost said I quit. Not to be ornery. Not because of him and his magnetism. But because of his devilish play. I couldn't handle it. It scared me. And now he'd called the damned thing *The Engagement Party*. Could he already have learned that Rusty had asked me to marry him? So far, in the script, I was Wade's fiancée. Who knows what the next rewrite would contain? I didn't want to stick around and find out.

"I'm going to work on my play for the rest of the month. Call these people"—he gave me a list—"and tell them I'm unavailable until June."

"Including your mother?"

"No, I am always available to her. She needs me. I'm the only one she has now. Rusty refuses to give her a number where he can be reached. My stepfather has become completely remote. And Lia is in her own world." He narrowed his eyes. "Then there is Lily," he said grimly.

"Oh, how right he is," said Mrs. DeRosa, slamming the front door and calling from the hall, sounding like a bird, high in a tree, but not a songbird, a bird of prey.

"Except for Wade and Lily," she cawed, entering the office, "everyone has abandoned me. And Lily has drawn lines. Wade, did I tell you Lily has drawn lines and says I can call only during certain hours?"

"I suppose she has to sleep sometime," he said in that brutal joking tone he used with her, jaw clenched, biting off the words.

She shrugged off her wraps and sat down. She looked bad. Ill kempt. She smelled bad too. Her hair was snarled. She was definitely on a downslide. She looked like a junkie.

"Sleep? Why? She doesn't have to go to work. How much sleep does she need? Anyhow, I am talking about daylight hours. These *certain hours* are daylight ones."

110

"She comes to see you every day," Wade reminded her.

"Yes, yes, I know." She brushed aside that ongoing act of good nature. "But now she has these sacrosanct hours and the queer thing is that those are the hours I often can't find your father. Do you think he would ever see Lily on his own, without me? She is my own special friend. . . ."

"Forget it."

"But the hours!"

"Fuck the hours."

"Rome, what do you think? What would you suppose if your husband didn't love you anymore, never embraced you, rarely talked to you, and, corresponding to that situation, your friend establishes hours she can't be disturbed, the same hours I can't find Milton. Rome? Rome?"

I sighed heavily. "I won't hear a word against Lily. She is my dear friend too. I've known her since I was a baby. Her husband and my father were best friends. I looked her up the other day. She's like a mother to me."

They both stared at me. Wade said dryly, "Another remarkable coincidence in the life of Rome Morrison."

"Life is so full of such coincidences," I said, "that you can almost call it a plan. I call it a pattern in a tapestry. Our life is made of many strings connecting to different people who are connected to each other so it seems to me that by the end of life, the weaving of these strings would form—"

"Go ahead and make these calls, okay. We'll talk about strings later."

They went into Wade's bedroom, Mrs. D saying, "It seems like *all* her strings are going to our family . . ." Then I could hear only the murmur of her voice occasionally overlaid by Wade's biting tone that sought to stem the flow of her woes, her needs, her chronic dismay, but had no more effect than teeth biting water and made no impression no matter how hard he bit down.

When I was through for the day I went to the bedroom

111

door to announce my departure. Wade was stretched out on the bed asleep. Mrs. D sat slumped forward, her hands in the air, palms up. Her eyes were fixed on them but looked inward.

"Mrs. DeRosa, shall I call you a cab?"

"To take me back to an empty house?"

"Well . . ."

She looked at me and her eyes focused. "Will you tell Rusty to please, please, please come see me?"

I didn't want to say hell no, I won't. So I said, "Well . . ." again. Great word. Sounds like you're thinking but you're not.

All this time her hands were out in front of her as if she were sunbathing her palms.

"They all hate me." She began her lament again. "Wade too. But at least he is trying to be kind. The others have given up trying."

"I think they all love you a lot, Mrs. DeRosa."

"I can't help being the way I am. If it's a nightmare for them, think how it is for me."

"It must be just awful," I said feelingly.

She looked surprised, even laughed a little, said, "Yes, awful."

"Is there anything you can take to feel better?"

"Yes, thank God there is. I can get relief for a little while. And sometimes there are quite nice dreams. Still, I'd be better off dead. Especially if Milton is in love with Lily, which deep in my heart, I know he is. Poor man. Why should I begrudge him a little happiness? But I do. If it's true, I'll kill myself, because I can't live without him."

She held out her hands piteously. "I'm afraid to touch anything. Wade broke a glass and it has gotten on everything."

Sure enough, there was a broken glass on the floor. She must have been asking Wade if there was a chip on it and he, at wit's end, decided to show her what a chipped glass was like in real life. But of course she couldn't perceive it correctly. One time I was on a ship and they blew out the stack to clean it. It belched brown smoke and all these horrible little grits and smuts drifted down like burnt rain. That's what Mrs. D thought happened when a glass broke. The air filled with splinters and shards, drifted down, got on everything.

She began to interrogate me keenly as to how much glass from the breakage could have gotten into her system through her different bodily apertures.

"None!" I swore, one hand over my heart, the other raised.

"I can feel it on my face and hands."

"None got in, Mrs. D."

"In the corners of my eyes, like sleepers, only going in instead of coming out . . ."

"None. None."

"Please look into my nose. I can feel them clustered . . ."

I knew if I once looked in her nose, there'd be worse to come. Luckily, before I began to gibber, Wade woke up and I turned her terrors over to him. I got dustpan and broom and did the best I could while Wade strong-armed her out of the house. He was putting her in a cab as I left.

TEN

I was glad to have the apartment to myself when I went home. After a light supper, I wrote for a few hours, then took off to spend the night with Rusty. He was staying in a borrowed apartment which was walking distance away. It was a beautiful night with a half moon lighting up the Bay as if it were keeping a promise it made when it was full— that this month, even though it diminished, its light wouldn't. The air was coldish. No matter how warm the days got in this city, the nights were always cool.

I thought how wonderful it was to be going to spend the night with my lover, he waiting for me, full of the same happy anticipation. I would tell him the details of my day just as I used to do when we first met, only now he was conscious and could make comments.

I remembered how glad I was when he couldn't see me or hear me and be critical, but the fact was, he wasn't critical of me—he thought I was wonderful.

As it happened, we didn't have much conversation until morning. There was so much loving to explore and we were still such amateurs and tended to get overexcited. This time we were a little more relaxed because more familiar and because we'd pledged our love and troth.

We undressed each other slowly, slowly as if we were the last present on Christmas but got so excited we had our orgasms outside of each other, still half-clothed. Undressed and in bed, the next time was long and sweet. We were enveloped in a fragrant miasma distilled from our kisses and juices through which our moans rose eerily. Through the open window, the moon beamed in its stardusty light.

This was our first full night together. We wrapped up in each other's arms and slept like stones. I awakened once, exulting in his loving grasp. I listened adoringly to his even breath, felt his soft red pelt against my skin and bones. It was heaven, just like the love songs always said. This was it. This was the right way to live and to sleep, being a pair of people. And we'd have babies too and love them so much that they'd grow up full of health, full of fun. They'd be known as the laughing children. Those DeRosas, people would say with wonder, they're always laughing. They're so happy. I never saw anything like it. They all love each other so much.

Now that I had once slept in my lover's arms, I would in the future, when sleeping by myself, experience a loneliness never known before. But, if all went well, and why shouldn't it, we would have almost all our nights together from now on, the ones apart being temporary and sporadic, only enhancing the joy of the next night's re-embrace.

In the morning, Rusty cooked breakfast for me. Happily, he announced that he had told his father about our secret engagement and that Milton wanted us to come to dinner. Yes, just a small dinner, he said. Only family. The others in the family need not even be told about the engagement if I did not wish it.

"Couldn't we just have dinner alone somewhere with your father?" I asked plaintively, but Rusty said no, how would they explain such a thing to his mother? No, it would be at their house, their cook would prepare the meal, and there would be seven of us.

116

"Seven!" I cried. It was sort of like Mrs. D's cawing sound.

"Why, yes. You and me, Dad and Mom, Wade, Lia, and Lily."

"Lily! Why Lily?" More cawing.

"Because she is such a close friend. She is like family and Mom is always at her best when Lily is around."

"I don't want to come," I said flatly, and he appeared so crestfallen, it hurt me to look at him.

How could I explain my attitude, since it was all based on Wade's play and I was sworn to secrecy. Secrecy was one thing I fully respected. Maybe the only thing. Well, truth, of course. I respected truth and wanted to live in it, but what was it really? Would I ever come close to the thing?

Even if I did explain my fears to Rusty, would he credit them? It helped me to imagine what he would say. It would be along the lines of: So my brother has begun a play about a deadly engagement party. Granted that is a strange coincidence, but didn't you once say life is so full of coincidences that the word scarcely applies? (I'd told him my tapestry theory.) Yes, I would reply, but I feel this play is a blueprint for something that is going to happen, that he *means* to happen. At first I thought it was a rehash of something that did happen, but now I know he is arranging a murder for someone in your family, by someone in your family, and therefore it is a bad idea to bring the family together for any reason whatsoever.

But I couldn't say anything, and anyhow Rusty was still talking. "It is so important to me. Please do it for my sake. To please me. It will be the last time we'll all be together. For me it is a farewell party too. Rome, I think the reason I came back was so I could make a real farewell instead of running away like a whipped dog. I even think the entire family should break up and not see each other anymore. We're not good for each other. Together our behavior gets

117

worse even though we think that the only way to survive is to hang on to each other with all our might. I want to tell them that I have started a new life for myself in another town and they can too! He got a messianic look. "Even Lia could join some group of special—"

"There is nothing wrong with Lia. She is the smartest and healthiest of you all."

Rusty smiled lovingly at me, melting my heart. "Say you'll come."

"I'll come."

"Daddy, it's Rome."

This was a week later, the day of the Engagement Party. I'd been several days getting hold of him this time, finally finding him in Nice.

During the week I'd seen Rusty every night and we loved each other more by the hour, by the minute. I'd gone every day to work for Wade, but he had not shown me his new work on the script. I'd gotten a paycheck, paid the rent, paid back Lily.

My own writing staggered to a stop. I still wrote on my novel, but since at night I threw away what I wrote in the morning, it pretty much amounted to a stoppage. Still, I knew that even if I'm stopped I have to keep going and soon the words will start to sing and I won't have to throw them away, not all of them. Coleridge was right. It's hard to create and be anxious as hell at the same time.

I was also losing all the weight I was gaining from loving Rusty, but like my writing it too held constant. Gaining and losing were equal, so what I had at the end of the day was the same. Sort of like Sisyphus pushing the rock up the hill each day and having it roll down at sunset, only with me it wasn't hard on the back, it was just a lot of time spent, time wasted.

"What is it this time?" Daddy asked ungraciously, being

in a different mood than last call. Chefs are notoriously moody. In fact, Daddy's a unique one in that he never took a knife to anyone or hit them with a pot. He never gets in a temper, but while most people have three or four moods, his range from sweet to sour with a hundred flavors in between. With two such parents—Mother with her fits, Daddy with his intricate moods, it's understandable I grew up unnoticeable, almost invisible.

"Daddy, I'm going to this dinner party at the DeRosas' tonight and I'm so scared I can't see straight. And I can't even tell you why. I just know something awful is going to happen. The family all hate each other for one reason or another. I don't know all the reasons. I guess Wade hates Rusty because he's such a darling and everyone always loved him the most. And Mrs. D is a maniac and Mr. D might be having an affair with Lily, our Lily, which, if so, they all know about and then the fact is I had a little go-around myself with Wade before I knew I loved Rusty and finally there's Lia, who won't talk to anyone except in her own language—"

"Stop!" he commanded. "It doesn't make any sense to me. Run it by me again slowly."

After I did so, he pondered, then said, "Don't worry. Go to the party. Stand by Rusty. It's only a party, not a prison term, not a battle. Listen. Here is what Dostoevsky said after hearing himself sentenced to hard labor: 'Life is everywhere life. I am not dismayed. Life is in ourselves, not in outward things. There will be people beside me and to be a man among men and remain a man forever, not to falter or fail in any misfortune whatever—that is what life is. That is where the task lies.' "

"Wow! That's great. Hold on while I write it down."

After I had done so, he continued. "Now, Rome, you have the misfortune of having to attend this dinner party

119

with all these awful people, two of whom you love as much as anyone in the world . . ."

"Three counting Lia, who is my friend m Gromy I've told you about."

"Three out of seven is pretty good, and if Lily loves Mr. DeRosa, he must be a good chap, so that's four, and you must like Wade somewhat to have had your little go-around. Five. There's you. You're okay. So it seems like there's only one person to fear, the maniac mother, and you're used to that sort of thing. So, there will be good people beside you. Life is everywhere life, even at a dinner party. Also, Lily has always had the knack of keeping things peaceable. Have fun. That's the main idea. That's what I always try to do."

The man was too wonderful for words. He always made me feel better, every time, bar none. He always knew what to say even when he was in a sour one of his hundred moods.

After this call to Daddy, I wasn't exactly looking forward to my engagement party but, well, I knew where the task lay.

Rusty and I got a taxi to his parents' house since they lived at the tiptop of Pacific Heights. We lay back against the seat, spineless and bleary-eyed from our week of love. If anything, Rusty had been more thrilled than me to discover sex, and we'd been going at it tooth and nail. We'd taken the nooner to new heights even with the nighter and morn-inger not so far behind. Just now we'd made love while getting dressed for the party, probably afraid the party was going to cut into our nighter. I didn't see why we couldn't have a partier too, a good noisy one. It might take Wade's mind off killing someone.

Unlike the play, it was not a stormy night, it was not autumn, nor did Rusty wear an Armani suit, although it was a very nice one. His brawny body wasn't made for suits.

He looked like he was busting out of them. I wore a black, high-necked, long-sleeved, ankle-length dress, my sole ornament being an outrageous diamond bracelet left to me by the hanged one.

Regardless of knowing where the task lay and that life was everywhere life, I felt my anxiety rise concomitant with the taxi's climb to the Heights. "Rusty," I said, "no matter what happens tonight, or after tonight, always know that I love you. These two weeks with you, conscious and unconscious, have been the happiest of my life. You are a dear man, a generous lover. You have made me feel loved, which I thought I never would feel, and you showed me that I can be a lover myself, which I also thought was not in my stars."

"God bless the lamppost," he said, "for bringing us together."

The cab dropped us in front of a large white stucco house with an imposing colonnaded entrance including low, sweeping steps. As we climbed them, Rusty asked, "Are you all right."

"I'm fine."

"You're walking funny." He looked upset.

Lia opened the door to us. In the background, Mrs. D was screaming just like in Wade's opening scene. "We're a little early," Rusty said to me. "Mom hasn't finished screaming.

"Is anyone with her?" he asked Lia. She shook her head in a negative. "I'll go," he said, "and help her dress." He kissed me. "I'll be right back."

I linked arms with Lia and she took me into the living room, which featured big fat contemporary furniture on ancient carpets. It was warm, colorful, comfortable, lots of mirrors, pretty sconced lights, and twinkling chandeliers. There were three large moody paintings by the same moody artist, sort of Whistlerish.

Even with the background screams, it was an inspiriting

atmosphere. My spirits lifted. My heart rose from my ankles, where it had plunged when Rusty said I was walking funny. Although it rose jerkily like an old elevator—those ones where you have to pull on the cable to get it going. The elevator man has to wear a leather gauntlet. Boston still has some of those in the seedier buildings.

There was a fire in the hearth, crackling and spitting exuberantly. By the time we reached it, the screams had ceased.

Wade walked in from a rear door, shimmering with beauty. He wore jeans, a black T-shirt, a tan cashmere jacket. Lia was dressed the same way, only with red hightop sneakers instead of two-hundred-dollar loafers. He kissed us both quite sweetly. "My sisters," he said.

While I was integrating that one, Mr. Milton DeRosa came in and Wade introduced me, saying, "Dad, this is Rome Morrison, my fiancée."

"Hello, Rome, we met at Lily's, I believe."

"Yes, we did. Nice to see you again."

"But you are not really Wade's fiancée, are you?"

"No, I'm Rusty's."

I cut my eyes to Wade, who definitely had gotten a big jolt. He hadn't known. I truly meant to keep it secret but couldn't resist throwing Wade off balance especially after his trick introduction.

"That's what I thought," Milton said. "I'm very pleased," he said formally. He kissed me, but it wasn't sweetly and he didn't say *daughter.*

I smiled at Lia and whispered, "Sisters." She lit up.

I grinned at Wade. Looking mean, he bared his teeth back at me, asking, "What is the matter with your leg? It's dragging."

At that moment Lily walked in and kissed us all. Milton told her it was an engagement party, and she said to me, "Darling! I'm so happy for you!"

Then Mrs. D rushed in, a gorgeous green dress whirling about her as if she had spontaneously combusted into green flames. She ignored us all and addressed her husband, "Did you say you met Rome at Lily's?"

It didn't seem even slightly possible that she could have heard our exchange. Quickly I said, "Mrs. DeRosa, did Rusty tell you we are engaged?"

Rusty, behind her, looked surprised and pleased that I'd decided to spread the word.

"Oh dear," she said. "I thought you were engaged to Wade. Wade, didn't you tell me you and Rome were . . ."

At this, Rusty's surprised look was intensified as his pleasure dimmed.

We were only ten minutes into the dinner party and already it was completely out of hand. I sat down before both legs started to drag.

The trouble with bringing people you know together is that they get to share information purposely withheld from some of them.

"Wade refers to all his girls as fiancées," Lily reminded her. "I think it's rather sweet of him."

"But I never was," I told them firmly, seeking to reassure Rusty. "I work for Wade, but I'm Rusty's fiancée. Those are the facts." I wondered if I was going to get a drink pretty soon. Unfortunately, no one ever kept rum in their house, and yet it seemed ill-bred of me to bring my own bottle— ill bred and desperate. I did have a lime in my purse, because it was always so heartbreaking if someone did have rum but then no lime.

Milton handed me a dark drink, almost black, with a piece of lime bobbing on the surface, looking like it had gotten into this swamplike drink by some horrendous bartending error. "Rusty says you drink rum. This is a dark rum. I hope it's all right."

Hoping so too, I said, "Thank you," and, in the same

123

motion of receiving it from his hand, carried it to my ardent lips.

"I didn't even know you worked for Wade!" Lily said. "Is that how you met Rusty?"

"Don't you know the lamppost story?" Mrs. D asked.

Everyone began to tell some version of the lamppost story. Lily, of course, did know, from me, about it, but hadn't learned it was Rusty. And the others hadn't known, as she did, how I had sat by his bed. And of course only Rusty knew how I'd released him from his coma, Rusty and the entire staff of Pacific Hospital.

He told them. "She awakened me with a kiss," he said, "a reverse *Sleeping Beauty.*" (Reverse was right!) They gushed over the romance of it.

"So you didn't know each other before?" Mrs. D asked. "Wade and I thought you must have or—"

"Or why would you have turned to look at her," Wade finished. He'd been very quiet throughout the hubbub of storytelling.

"You were singing!" Rusty burst out. "I've just remembered, Rome! You were singing and I thought it was so wonderful especially because . . ."

He blushed.

I finally got to see his famous blush.

Scarlet is not a strong enough word to describe the color he turned, and he became not merely transformed but transmogrified. His features twisted and changed. He turned still as stone and his tongue even protruded. It was like a fit only a frozen one. He looked like a gargoyle.

Everyone delicately looked away from him and at one another, waiting politely for it to pass as they must always have done down through the years.

Except me. I jumped up and stumbled over to him as if on a pitching deck. I threw my arms around him and kissed his horrible countenance.

It lasted only a minute and then he was himself again. The dear, sweet lines of his face were recreated, restored, and familiar. My heart was hammering with fright at suddenly not recognizing him.

"But what were you going to say," Wade insisted. "She was singing and you thought it was so wonderful especially because . . . because what?"

"Because she was a cripple." He turned to me anxiously. "Rome, I'm sorry. I thought you were a cripple. That's not why I turned though. I turned because you were singing away despite the fact and I thought it was so splendid of you. So brave!"

Lily said, "Why on earth would you think such a thing? Rome has never been in the least crippled. She has a beautiful walk."

Wade said, "She was crippled that week."

The incredibly embarrassing scene in the post office flashed before my eyes. The gigantic sob story, including the plight of the poor cripple.

If he mentioned so much as one word about it, there *would* be a murder tonight. His. By me. Something he hadn't considered in his play, that he wouldn't get to finish it due to his own sudden dinner-party death.

I glared at him but he didn't say a word. I knew him well enough by now to know he got his satisfaction out of seeing me remember the P.O., imagining the feelings it engendered.

I was still standing by Rusty, his arm around my shoulders, mine around his waist. The main thing was not to move and show that I was crippled again. The main thing was not to sing either, or sob. What I had to do was to get back to my drink in one piece or, even better, get it over to me.

"I'm so glad you remembered at last," I said to Rusty. I sank down in the nearest chair. Lia was bringing me my

125

drink. She knew. As usual, she hadn't missed a trick. She knew about the P.O. scene too. She knew everything. And she was on my side. She would protect me from . . . from . . . well, the other side.

She hadn't once stared into the fire as Wade had her dimwittedly do in the script and which I began to do now as I ceased being the center of attention and different ones chitchatted together. I think I purposely sent myself into a stupor. Maybe it was a reaction from the frenzy of the first twenty minutes of the party when I'd been a nervous wreck, culminating in the adrenaline rush over Rusty's unparalleled blush. I'd had it. I was exhausted. I no longer knew where the task lay. Sorry, Dad. Sorry, Dostoevsky. Sorry, Your Honor.

ELEVEN

When dinner was announced, I made it to the table all right. If my leg was dragging, no one commented, not even Wade. There didn't seem to be any telltale track on the rugs.

First course was a lemony sorrel soup, a green salad with designer lettuce vinaigrette. Then came a butterflied leg of lamb, a little underdone for my taste, with roast potatoes and carrots that were perfect. The California wines were tasty and Milton didn't hold back—the table was littered with bottles.

It was a good meal and everyone was in a good mood. There were affectionate congratulatory toasts. Everything was going to be all right. I'd been a fool to get so exercised about this party.

Rusty also relaxed and shelved his idea of lecturing the family to all go their separate ways and never see each other again.

Even when Wade served the coffee, helped by Lia, I didn't panic. Everything went smoothly. The family laughed and chatted. Nobody died. Nobody keeled over. No one said they felt funny. Mrs. D didn't even ask if there was a chip on the cup, made no lamentations. It was all normal as normal. We could have been a Midwest farm family celebrating a corn-stuffed silo. And now it was almost over and Rusty and I could begin the rest of our lives.

When we rose from the table, I came out of the warm security of my mindless stupor to notice the coffee cups. All of them were drained to the dregs except mine and Milton's, which were untouched and Rusty's, which was half drained.

Back in the living room the fire had lost its exuberance and now seemed almost to be sobbing, so diminished was it, so subdued. Where the flames had leapt, they now cowered and crept. The crackling and whistling had subsided to an occasional pitiful *pfft* sound. No one seemed inclined to restore it to its former glory, and although cognac was poured, the party seemed to be over. The rest of the room seemed different to me too. The moody paintings were now glowering. The beautiful carpets just made me think of all the young Asians who had gone blind making them, and the plump furniture signified the overstuffed class of people who sat in it.

Before we left, Mrs. D clutched my arm, pulled me aside, and whispered tremulously, "Did Milton say he met you at Lily's?"

I was in a spot, a tight one, up against a wall, which is where she in fact had me. What I had going for me was that she couldn't trust her own senses, so I cravenly played on this weakness saying, "I don't think you heard right."

"Well, then, where *did* you meet him?"

"I met him here tonight." Which was true.

"For the first time?" she pressed me.

"Yes," I said. It was the first time here.

If ever there was a time for a white lie, this was it. My mother used to define a white lie as one told with the intent to deceive someone who has no right to know the truth. Perhaps Mrs. D had the right, but it would unhinge her. She knew the truth already, but she wanted it confirmed and I wasn't going to confirm it. Not me. Let Lily or Milton be the confirmer.

"Please let go of my arm."

She unloosed me, then scrutinized her hand to see if she'd gotten glass on it from my silk sleeve.

"Lily is good as gold," I said. "Which you well know. She would not do anything to hurt anyone, especially people she loves."

"She loves Milton."

"She loves this family. She has no family of her own. You are lucky to have her in your life."

"Why don't I feel lucky?"

I was startled. She looked me straight in the eye as she said this and her demeanor was sane as sane. I hated myself for the patronizing way I'd been talking to her. So I said, "I met your husband at Lily's one afternoon a couple of weeks ago."

"Thank you."

The next morning when I arrived at Wade's, letting myself in with the key he had given me, he was on the telephone in the living room. He dropped it with a clatter, threw back his head, and let loose an anguished cry. At first I thought, hoped, it was some Wadian performance for my benefit, but the cry chilled me, rent me. It had to be real, coming as it did from his entrails, tearing raggedly through his chest, his thrown-back neck, out the rictus of his mouth.

He wailed, gasped, wrackingly sobbed. His body jerked around the room like a berserk wind-up toy. Tears splattered out of his eyes and ribbons of mucus fell from his nose. I ran for a towel, no mere handkerchief could stanch the flow, and I mopped away at him as he continued his wounded cries.

"Wade, what? Tell me? Please!"

"Dead. Mom. Killed herself. Milton just found her."

I began to cry with him, crying for my own suicided mother at last, for I'd not shed one tear for her, not one.

We clasped each other like drowning men rocked back and forth in a violent sea, drenched by salty waves of combined tears.

"Oh, Mother," I howled above Wade's wails, "I did love you. I did. I'm sorry. Forgive me. I miss you. I will never forget you. I will always grieve for your terrible suffering. Can you hear me? Can you hear me?"

We lay in each other's arms, quiet now, sodden with grief. Wade's head was on my chest. I thought he was sleeping. His hand pushed up my shirt, took hold of my breast. He began to suckle my nipple like a baby, sucking, sucking, sucking. I wondered if he had retrogressed, thought I was his mother. I let him do it. Why not if it helped, if it could get him over this, the first worst hour. It's only a nipple and it felt nice for me too. He wasn't sucking hard, not trying to drag milk from the poor thing, just sweetly sucking with soft lips or sometimes just sort of pushing at it with his tongue. He switched to the other breast, and it was the same thing and it was nice. After a while his cock slipped inside me as if it were just by chance that it had gotten all swelled up while he thought he was nursing and I have to say I was ready, my vagina, that is, ready as could be, lathered, swollen, pulsing, and waiting to receive whatever might come her way by chance like a big, swollen, grief-stricken dick. I didn't care. Again it felt nice. I wasn't detached exactly, but I wasn't all there either. I don't know where I was. We didn't move, just lay there swollen together. Every so often he'd give a little thrust, like a message, and we'd moan and maybe I'd pull at him a little with my vagina muscle and we'd moan. Then we put our tongues in each other's mouths and let them lie in there while we took air in and out of our nostrils to stay alive, our bodies

lying there as if they were dead except for the little inside
thrustings and tuggings, except for the moanings in our
throats, and the air drafts through our noses, time going on,
time passing in this way until came this long, agitated,
wrenching, aching orgasm that was the final sob of our
grief.

We lay there some more, drenched with our sweat and
tears, maybe slept a little, finally separated, two wet rags,
and our clothes in little sopping piles on the floor. Wade
went to the shower, but I didn't follow, went instead to the
kitchen sink and sponged myself, using a dish towel. Then,
from the laundry, I got a pair of his blue jeans and a white
sweatshirt to put on, and waited in the kitchen for what
would happen next, feeling my brain start to think about
things and wishing it wouldn't. I went to the fridge and
poured a glass of wine from a half-full bottle, turned, and
bumped into Wade, reaching for a beer. He too was dressed
in jeans and a white sweatshirt. We both said, "Hi."
    Standing in the kitchen, him against the fridge, me
against the sink, we looked at each other out of eyes that
were a hundred years old.
    "Do you love Rusty?" he asked.
    "Yes."
    "You were my girl first."
    "Not really."
    "If you loved him, you wouldn't be able to do what you
just did."
    "We were only crying."
    "You love me."
    "Can I borrow these clothes?"
    "Sure. Will you tell Rusty how you happen to be wearing
them?"
    "Maybe. Do you want me to work today?"
    "No."

"I'm sorry about your mother, Wade. My mother committed suicide too."

"I know. I heard you calling out to her." He threw the empty beer bottle across the room to the trash basket. "Life is shit."

I didn't say anything. Maybe it was. Death sure was.

"You're fired," he said.

I stayed silent, not thinking it over, or anything over, because I still was trying not to think, just trying to field what he threw my way as best I could. I just stood there being as colorless as I could.

"Get out of here."

I went.

That night, Rusty being with his father and sister, I had dinner with Nancy, whom I'd scarcely seen in the past ten days. It was good to talk with her. I realized how nice it must be for normal women who can tell everything to their friends. *Confide,* I guess the word is. I wondered how much of my inability to confide was simply fear of not being loved if they knew the truth about me, or how much was not wanting to lose the image of me I wanted them to have because if they lost it, maybe I'd lose it too.

It seemed to me that if I could just be myself, whatever that was, it would be so freeing! Also, if I could just say whatever was on my mind, then, among other things, maybe I could find out what lurked there, hiding out in all the different lobes. Writing did the job to some extent. Sometimes I wrote a line that was so startlingly true, it shone. Maybe if I was able to confide, I couldn't write.

Roast chicken, salad, a bottle of white, a crusty loaf, and Nancy and I were chowing down by candlelight so the green of the apartment retreated into a seeming of a dreaming jungle foliage. We could almost hear the thin calls of

132

night birds mingling with monkey laughs and the coiling rustle of the sinuous python.

"I wonder if she actually ended by taking a drink of the ground glass she'd so frantically feared," I told Nancy in awed tones. "As if it were a relief to finally get it over with and die of it and stop being perpetually engaged in glass guerrilla warfare."

"Where do you even get ground glass?" Nancy wondered. "Or how do you grind it? Will there be a post-mortem?"

"I don't know. There was an empty Xanax bottle, a note. It seems pretty clear-cut."

"What did the note say?" Nancy was big-eyed with curiosity.

"It's terrible. The suicide note said, 'Darling Milton, now you and Lily need not have your *certain* hours together, you can have all the hours you want, unburdened by me and my suffering. Maybe you'll remember our happy times . . .'

"Rusty says," I interjected, "there were no happy times, that he never saw them happy together once."

"Was that it? Was that the whole note?"

"No. It goes on." I quoted from memory. " '. . . Maybe you'll remember our happy times and soon die of boredom with Lily just as Rome will with Rusty, who is so much like you.' "

"God, what a bitch!" Nancy shrieked.

"Then she wrote: 'I'm leaving Wade all my money, as he's the only one who loved me from start to finish. To you I leave Lia, her hateful looks and sullen scowls . . .' "

"Imagine describing your own daughter that way!" Nancy shrieked again with outrage, coming as she did from a loving family.

"I suppose it's how Mother would have described me," I admitted.

"They're all better off without her," Nancy steamed. "She

133

hated everyone but Wade." Then she added acutely, "What's amazing is that she decided to relinquish her hold on them all. What made her finally give up, do you suppose?"

"Probably knowing she had lost Milton. And Rusty too. First Rusty, then Milton. Or maybe first Lia. Lia went into her own world. Rusty went to Chicago. Milton found solace in Lily's love. There was no one left but Wade, who loved her incredibly, but, having to take the entire brunt of her neuroses, had constantly to keep himself from killing her."

"Do you think he did kill her?" Nancy whispered with big round eyes. I began to wish she'd blink.

"No. I saw his grief." I paused, getting up my nerve. "Nancy . . ."

"What? Well, come on, spit it out."

"Just before I left the engagement party, I told Mrs. DeRosa I'd seen Milton at Lily's."

"Do you think it *mattered,* that it might have decided her?"

"I don't know. She asked me about it and I waffled and then it seemed so demeaning not to give her a straight answer. I believe she really wanted to know, didn't want to be lied to, and I wanted to be truthful. So I was. Maybe it killed her. Maybe it was the final straw that broke the camel's back. And with her it would be something as light as a straw, as light as a chip or a shard."

"Poor Rome," Nancy commiserated.

"I told Rusty about it. He said when he went to help her get ready for the party and calm her down from her crying fit, there was pen and paper already out at her desk with the writing begun."

"Was she crying before dinner because she'd had a scene with Milton?"

"I guess so. Then she was so calm all through dinner that I think her mind was made up."

134

"I never heard anything like this."

"You still haven't heard the worst of the note. She said, 'With Rome in the family, I leave a worthy successor, one who will cause misery to you all.'"

"God!" Nancy stood up and threw down her napkin. She stomped around the room and returned to the table. "Was that because of your telling her about Milton?"

I sighed. "I don't think so. I'm sure it was because she knew Wade and I had been lovers before I was with Rusty. Then, I didn't tell you this, but I quit on him and Mrs. D came and specially asked me not to leave him. So I did go back to work for him but I left him for Rusty just the same. I think what she was really asking of me was to love him."

"I never heard anything like this," Nancy said again, shaking her head dolefully. "Tell me, does Rusty know you were . . . uh, with Wade?"

"No, I haven't told him, although at the party Mrs. D said something about me and Wade that I could see made him wonder."

"Maybe you should tell him, Rome. It all happened before you loved him and it would sort of clear the boards. Since you're going to be married, it's good to start out truthful so you can keep on that way."

Nancy was right, but it hadn't "all" happened so long before as she thought. It was the same day I'd kissed Rusty awake, and Rusty felt so thrilled and romantic about that kiss, it seemed to me it would kill him to know I'd been with Wade that very morning and that the whole "kiss" had occurred only because I'd been curious to see another penis and got carried away.

Then of course it had "all" happened again this very day. I honestly felt it didn't count because we'd been insensible with grief at the time, but it sure would count to Rusty, it would destroy him, and I had a suspicion that it counted a little to Wade, that he didn't see us as being so insensible as

135

we were. But it wasn't Rome and Wade who combined this morning, it was just two people crying themselves into a four-legged beast of sorrow.

This was what I needed most to confide to Nancy but I couldn't. Learning this, her shriek of *God!* would cease to do the job. Words would fail her. She'd look at me as if I *were* a worthy successor to Mrs. D, and what a judgment that was, a penalty even Your Honor wouldn't think of; a life sentence of filling the place of that mad woman, becoming hated by all who now loved me.

"Nancy, I feel like she's put a curse on me. Maybe I should get out of the family while I can, before I do harm. I have such a fear anyhow of becoming a crazy woman like Mother. I always figured I'd be okay if I didn't have kids and if I died before I was thirty, just writing hard the whole time, but here I am not even twenty . . ."

"Now, just stop that talk. You're not making sense. Rusty loves you and he's a complete sweetheart. I only thought it would be good to be frank with him, but if it scares you, don't. See, she just wrote that note to leave everyone feeling rotten, and she has. She wanted to keep her control going. Don't do her the favor of crumbling."

"I was at Wade's when he got the news. He cried himself inside out and, Nancy, guess what, I cried too. For Mother. I never cried for her before. I even told her I loved her."

"Maybe she heard."

I knew Nancy would say that, wanted her to, even though it was ridiculous.

"She always used to ask me to tell her I loved her. I'd do it to keep the peace, not because I meant it. I don't know how she got any gratification from such a forced avowal. Anyhow, today I said it on my own."

"Would she tell you she loved you?"

"Yes, but she didn't mean it. It was part of the forcing process. Whereas Daddy means it even though"—I ducked my head, feeling strangely embarrassed—"even though he never says it."

"I love you," Nancy said.

"I love you too."

TWELVE

Did you hear about the villainous note?" I asked Lily when I saw her at her apartment the next morning.

"Yes." She sort of rolled her eyes, but I knew she wasn't going to speak ill of the dead. She only said, "She was a very unhappy woman."

We were in her kitchen that overlooked a backyard with a gnarled old apple tree, preternaturally bonsaied by lack of care and light, that yet was putting out sweet pale blossoms on a few of its arthritic old branches, doing its best to obey spring, the enforcer, and be productive. Maybe juicy apples wouldn't come of it, but it sure was pretty for now and made the barren blossoms more poignant.

Lily moved briskly around, making fresh orange juice and pouring boiling water over some mocha java grounds. All was shiny and neat: no grease spots, no errant crumbs.

I wondered if she felt at all guilty. I wondered if Milton did. I wasn't going to ask. Daddy said he didn't feel guilty about Mother's death. He said he'd done the best he could. I'm sure Milton did too. But when he saw a little love come his way, he couldn't resist. He just needed so much to be with someone normal and sweet, someone he could have a conversation with. Maybe he and Lily never even had sex together, they just liked to spend a little time, time that could be snatched from the harridan, certain hours.

Why did it seem worse if they did have sex? Why did it seem so bad that I did with Wade when it didn't have anything to do with not loving Rusty or not wanting to be with him. Life was sure tricky. But it wasn't shit. It was wonderful. Because it was so full of feeling. And there were so many kinds of feeling. I'd had no idea.

"Will you and Milton get married, Lily?"

"Yes, when a suitable time has passed."

"I'm happy for you. And for me too. You'll be my mother-in-law."

She laughed, sitting down next to me at the little kitchen table for two. "So I will." She kissed me. "An unexpected bonus."

"How's Milton doing?" The coffee was good, mellower than my French roast.

"He's very shaken. Rusty's being a great comfort to him. But Lia isn't well. I think she may have to be committed—"

I choked, splattering coffee. "What? What's this?"

"She's stopped talking entirely, won't eat, won't even move. She shrinks away from anyone trying to touch her."

"I'll care for her." I stood up. "She can come to stay with me."

"You have your job—"

"No, I don't. Wade fired me. I'll call Rusty."

"Do you think you should interfere?"

"Interfere, hell! She's my sister." I was already punching numbers on the wall phone. "Hi, Rusty? I'm at Lily's. She just told me about Lia. Let me take care of her in my apartment. Nancy's going to L.A for a few days and Wade fired me, so I'm free. The green will be good for her. So will I."

"That's sweet of you, Rome, but she needs professional help."

"No, she doesn't."

"Rome, honey. You don't really know Lia at all. You have this idea about her, this fantasy. You've sort of glamorized her. Forgive me, but I think in your mind you've let her replace your dad because you think you need a sage around. It's easy to project wisdom on someone who can't talk."

"Oh, really? Then maybe you should commit *me.*"

Rusty laughed, obviously not hearing the fury behind the remark.

"I'm coming to get her," I said, hanging up before he could make any more idiotic protestations.

The DeRosa place was ten blocks away. Traveling over hill and down dale as one does in San Francisco, I fetched up at the manse about twenty minutes later. Rusty met me at the door and gave me a big hug. "I love you," he said.

"I love you with all my heart forever and ever," I responded with a juicy kiss thrown in. "Until death do us part," I added.

"Just let him try."

"Where's Lia?"

"You're determined?"

"You bet."

She was crouched before the hearth exactly in the way Wade had described in his screenplay, as if cooking meat with her eyes, which in this case she'd have to do were there meat, since there was no fire. The scene could have chilled me, but I didn't let it. Instead, I went over, hunkered down beside her, took one of her hands in mine. She had beautiful hands, like her mother. "M Gromy," I said. I waited.

After a little while her hands grew warmer in mine and she looked at me, smiled tremulously, said, "M Gromy."

"Nancy's gone away for a few days and Rusty's awfully busy arranging the funeral. I'm lonely. Will you come stay with me? Wade fired me, so I don't have to go to work."

She stood up, which I took as an affirmative.

Rusty was in the hall when we came out hand in hand.

"Go get some things from your room, your box, and what-ever else you need," I told her. "I'll wait here."

Rusty watched her draggle off up the stairs. "Do you want me to drive you?" he asked.

"No, we'll walk. It's all downhill. Will you come by later?"

"I'm worried about Dad. I hate to leave him. His blood pressure's up and he's been having some pain. It's all such a shock. Not just her death but her will. It turns out the money was all hers. Even the store was hers. So now it's Wade's. Dad owned the house that the earthquake kicked over, but it wasn't quake insured. This house is rented. He doesn't have a bean. In fact, this last year he's gone into debt to keep up his life-style even though he drew a huge salary from the store. Now he doesn't even have a job."

"Surely Wade won't fire him."

"He's never liked Wade, you know. It's always been an armed truce between them."

"What a mess. But don't get sucked into his troubles, Rusty. You'd gotten away free. Stay free."

"That doesn't sound kind, Rome." His tone was gentle but I felt accused.

"I guess it doesn't," I said sheepishly although it wasn't at all like me to be sheepish.

"Didn't you stand by your dad?"

I tried to think if I had when my mother died. "I'm sure I was too wrapped up in myself. I guess I never worry about Daddy. It would be like worrying about Buddha."

"Why did Wade fire you?"

This was beginning to sound like an inquisition, like he was Your Honor instead of darling Rusty.

"Well . . . . I'll try to explain later."

"Will you look for another job?"

"I was going to . . . uh, just go to Chicago with you."

"Don't count on that for a while."

142

This sounded awfully brusque. At least it wasn't another question, it had that going for it, but it hurt me. I began to feel hurt along with sheepish. What a combination.

"The police are keeping the body for an . . . uh . . ."

"Autopsy?"

"Yeah. But we're having the funeral tomorrow, really a memorial service. You'll come?"

"Hell no. The woman cursed me in her suicide note."

"She's my mother, Rome. Won't you come for my sake?"

I seemed to remember that line from the occasion of my not wanting to go to the engagement party. That time it had melted my heart. This time it didn't.

"No. It's your funeral. I went to your engagement party."

"*My* engagement party?"

"Well, okay, ours," I grumbled.

Lia appeared and I went off without kissing Rusty good-bye. I felt like we'd had a fight although we hadn't exactly. I felt like we'd got unengaged, that he'd chosen Milton over me, although I know he was just being a good son. But he'd had it with being a good son. He'd wanted to disband the family, develop a bad streak. This was his chance and he wasn't taking it. Let Lily take care of Milton. The hell with waiting for a "suitable time."

But then there was Lia. Milton wasn't in any shape to take care of her, and Lily hadn't made any offers in that direction. Still, I was pretty sure Lia would be all right in a few days and then *she* could take care of Milton.

I wondered how long it would be before the postmortem results were in. I wondered if, inside her stomach, they'd find and piece together a set of china Rusty and I could use in our kitchen.

Lia walked along beside me, probably glad to be headed back to her neighborhood stand in front of the Alhambra, but I could tell she was depressed as hell. She was a woman with a natural inner glow and it was almost out, barely guttering. It seemed like my inner glow wasn't doing too well either. You'd think any kind of liquid would snuff it, but I had an idea the rum liquid and lime liquid would fan the flame to life.

I just hated it that Rusty made me feel sheepish. It made me not want to marry him. Especially if he already didn't want to marry me. It was hard to believe we'd greeted each other so joyfully and lovingly, then a short while later, only minutes!, parted the way we did, without a kiss. I couldn't even put my finger on what went wrong, what fell apart, except that *everything* I said sounded crummy—calling it *his* engagement party, *his* funeral, telling him to keep out of his father's troubles.

But how about Chicago and him saying "Don't count on it" so curtly? Or him saying, "That doesn't sound kind, Rome," making me feel like a rat, making me feel sheepish? Was that nice?

I left Lia out front and went up to pour a drink. Maybe this didn't constitute Taking Care of Lia, but it was a beginning. I was beginning by taking care of me.

I carried the drink down to the fountain. Already she had some of her cronies around and had even gotten up the energy to initiate one of her famous pantomimes. I laid my head back on the tiles and caught some rays of the afternoon sun, my eyes almost closed. Through the slits I saw Lia reach into the tiny watch pocket of her jeans and take out some imaginary thing that she held between her thumb and forefinger. Then with the other thumb and forefinger she made some small motion. Was it a watch? Was she winding a watch? No. No one carried watches in watch pockets. I closed my eyes and drowsed. What did you carry in those useless little pockets? They were mainly decorative, or like appendixes, not good for anything. I dozed off, giving my

144

glow a chance to expand in the sun while Lia methodically got her glow going by pantomiming away.

After a while the sun sent the shadow of the building my way and I woke up. We went to the apartment and freshened up to look nice for McDonald's, where we sumptuously supped. Back home, it was early to bed for Lia but not me.

I wrote on my novel but I wasn't concentrating.

I wanted to call Rusty to say I was sorry, but I couldn't think what I was sorry about. In New England we say, never let the sun set on a bad word. There was a feeling of bad words having passed between us, and the sun was just about down. I called him, but he wasn't home, so the sun went ahead and set on whatever it was. I wrote for a few more hours, then hit the sack.

In the morning the buzzer woke me up. "Who's there?" I asked the intercom. It said Moo and I buzzed whoever in, putting on my robe. It was Wade, wearing a black suit and a black shirt too, which seemed extreme. Lia kept on sleeping, face to the wall. I motioned him into the kitchenette and got some coffee going. "If you're thinking of hiring me back, forget it."

"I'm not." His tone was sepulchral. I looked at him. He was pale and still. He looked like a black and white photo of himself. The planes of his face stood out sharply against the drop of the frowsy cupboards, counters, and appliances. I felt like I was sharing coffee with a sculpture by Rodin.

"What's the matter?" I asked. Then I remembered his mother was dead and today was the funeral. "I'm sorry, Wade, I'm still half asleep."

"Milton's going to fight the will," he said.

"That's disgusting. People should be able to leave their money wherever they damn well want. I hate to see families fighting wills."

145

"He'll say she was non compos mentis. Mom would hate it. She always made a huge effort to appear normal outside the family. And she wasn't crazy, she just had all these obsessions and couldn't help herself."

"It's a shame. It's degrading of Milton to do it."

"It's a lot of money. I'd happily give half to Rusty and Lia, but I don't want him having any. Why the hell should he? He's been unfaithful to her for years and made her life a misery. She only wanted to be loved. By all of us, but especially him."

He choked. I hoped he wasn't going to cry. I wasn't up to it. I felt a huge wave of sympathy rolling out of me over to him. I had to dig deep to find my business voice. "Here's your coffee."

"Lily won't have him when she finds out he's broke, when she finds out it was all Mom's money."

At this, my sympathy wave, which was hovering and waiting to break like those Japanese prints of tsunamis, went down the drain. I replied peevishly, "That's a rotten thing to say. Lily is truer than true. I happen to know she deeply loves Milton."

The buzzer buzzed and I buzzed back without bothering to hear the moo. Lia seemed to have inched closer to the wall, as if determined not to wake up, no matter who or how many arrived.

It was Rusty. He too was dressed in black, only unlike Wade's designer number, his was a baggy suit that was probably someone else's. He was as pale as Wade, his freckles standing out as if he'd been spattered with terracotta.

He kissed me. I could feel Wade's glance grappling us.

"Lia and I aren't coming to the funeral," I reminded Rusty. "Want some coffee?"

"So who's going to testify to Mom's madness?" Wade

146

asked him without any greeting. "Lily? That will be a nice conspiracy."

"Dad's just upset. He doesn't know what he's doing or saying. I'm sure he can land another job with just as good pay and that will be that."

"Yeah, except at another job they'd maybe expect him to work and he doesn't know how. He just knows how to be Mr. Good Old Boy Around Town. Of course he could marry for money *again,* but that would be tough on old Lily, who's been so patient."

"Oh, Wade, shut up," I expostulated. "What's the point of unloading on Rusty? He feels just as bad as you. Worse, since she said those mean things about him and me in her note."

"No," said Rusty. "Wade feels worse. Because he loved her more."

"Here, have some coffee."

I refilled Wade's too. They drank quietly. I wiped the counters to try to make them look like Lily's. Then Rusty said, "Come on, Wade. Let's go."

He smiled and his eyes lit up a little. "I think there'll be a lot of people, Wade. You'll be surprised. She has so many friends from over the years, a lot of people who admired her for her beauty and gaiety and wit. Not so long ago"—Rusty turned to me, still smiling—"she was the most socially sought-after woman in town. Wade, you remember how full her calendar always was, how the phone would ring and ring and the flowers would come? It's only in the last few years that—"

"That everyone dropped her," Wade said savagely. "Starting with Milton."

". . . that she didn't *want* to go to parties anymore, or have them," Rusty finished. "That getting ready for a party, she'd cry . . ."

Rusty hung his head and a lone silver tear slipped down

147

his face, a perfect tear, a tear to hang from a miniature chandelier to light up a fairy palace. It glittered on his cheek. What an amazing difference between it and the paroxysm of Wade's lachrymose deluge.

"We'll come," I said suddenly, manically. "Lia and I will come."

I scuttled to Lia's bed and shook her awake although I knew she already was. "Get up. We're going with your brothers to the funeral. We'll forget the suicide note, written by a crazed woman not knowing what she was saying. We'll forgive her and mourn her and not be dismayed by our trouble like Dostoevsky said. Life is everywhere life, Lia."

What did Dostoevsky mean really? That life went on no matter what happened or where you were? What *was* life? Nothing, really. It was an illusion. It was only what one perceived. Well, of course it was also a tapestry.

"We'll stand by each other shoulder to shoulder." We actually were shoulder to shoulder at this point, as I had her on her feet, headed for the bathroom. Rusty and Wade were gaping at me from the kitchenette. I was trying to do for her what Daddy did for me, only it was a rush job. "We'll bravely see your mother into the ground—or into our memories, rather, since it's a memorial service, not a funeral. Forget about the ground."

Lia listened with wide eyes. "It's important for you to see all her friends who will come so you can remember her when she would go off to a party with a happy heart, more beautiful than anyone else, enchanting everyone in her path. And it's important to be reminded that we'll bite the dust pretty soon ourselves. I'll be twenty in two months and haven't finished my first novel. You'll soon be sixteen and haven't started on your English."

We washed our faces, combed our hair, me still buoying her up. "Life is short and we can't let horrible parents stop

148

us or get in our way by their living or dying. And we can't blame them either because it's all up to us. Come on, I'll lend you a dress."

I gave her Mother's brown linen dress and a pair of Nancy's shoes, as she had big feet and Lia's red hightops wouldn't do the job. I wore the black gown I'd worn to Rusty's engagement party. It looked plenty funereal without the diamond bracelet. Lia looked pretty. She had a nice figure if she wouldn't shamble. But that was up to her.

As the four of us walked to Wade's van, Rusty said, "Thank you, Rome. You're wonderful and I love you."

"I love you too, and I'm sorry about yesterday and the things you said."

He laughed and hugged me.

"I don't think Lia knew about Mom's note," Wade said when she went running ahead and couldn't hear.

"Well, she should know. It's about time you guys included her in things and talked to her like a human being."

"If your speech was an example," Wade retorted, "I wouldn't know how to begin. I never heard such gibberish in my life. How's she supposed to know who Dostoevsky is?"

"Lia *is* Dostoevsky."

"Yeah, and I'm Tolstoy," said Wade.

"I'm Jorge Luis Borges," I said wishfully, "and P. G. Wodehouse combined," picking two authors who got to live life for the longest time available, probably because they were the only two who weren't drunks.

The whole city turned out for Mrs. D's funeral, and it seemed like it did everybody good except maybe Milton, since it still didn't get him any of the inheritance and therefore maybe it didn't do Lily so much good either. It's funny how you can think everything will be just fine if only a certain person dies and it turns out not only not to be fine but worse than it was.

It did Lia the most good. She looked around, amazed and happy. It did enable her to see her mother in another light, to spark dim memories of Mrs. D in her glory years. Lia began to smile, which was inappropriate but good. When people got up and said nice things about her mom, Lia took in every word. She listened to the music and smelled the flowers. I could feel her consciousness expand out of the corner of her brain, where it had forlornly huddled. Talking was just around the corner, I knew. I already felt triumph for her. She was going to take on life and we were in each other's tapestry forever.

Lily and I had a quiet lunch together while the family received mourners at home. We went to Greens, a chi-chi Zen Buddhist vegetarian restaurant in Fort Mason which had been a WWII naval base and now was given over to the arts. We had bits of beans and greenery, seeds and thistles, flavorful chewable bread, and good white wine. We talked about the money.

"It's very distressing to me," Lily admitted. "I'd always believed it to be Milton's."

"But does it matter? I mean, why should it matter? It's just money. He's still Milton." I remembered originally wondering if he'd still be Milton if he was the janitor and now here it was, a viable question.

All around us, other people were talking about money. It didn't seem like a place for power lunches, but it was. I kept hearing words like *deadline* and *strategy* and sums in the six or eight figures.

"It matters on many levels," Lily answered thoughtfully. "I believed he'd built the department store into the success it is by his own hard work and initiative. Now it turns out she bought it for him to be head of. That's all right. I can accept that. Probably if he'd been a hard-driving workaholic, he wouldn't be the sweet, thoughtful, playful man that he is."

Lily paused to gently chew a leaf. I'd demolished my plate of food in seconds, which was okay since it gave me more time to drink. Out the windows I saw some giant class of sailing boats chasing one another around the bay. It looked like the America's Cup. They were so monstrously big and the sailors on them were so outsized, it looked as if they and their boats had fed on nuclear waste and become aberrants.

"But what really disturbs me," she went on, not looking disturbed because she's so naturally composed-looking, "is that all these years I thought he stayed with her because she was unwell and he felt obliged to care for her, which I understood and could accept. But"—she swallowed while an emotion like scared and vulnerable that I felt all the time shone in her eyes for a millisecond, like a signal light that had gone on by mistake—"but what if it was the money that kept him and what if he never intended to leave her and just used her illness as an excuse to me for his remaining?"

"What about Lia? He couldn't leave Lia in any case."

"We could always find a place for Lia."

I bowed my head as Rusty had done earlier that morning but not to let loose a perfect tear; it was to hide my fury. How could everyone be so wrong about Lia, even Lily! No sense expostulating. Everyone just ignored me when I did and started to treat me like they did her.

THIRTEEN

During the next days I spent most of my time writing and reading. I had a stack of books of fabulous contemporary writers who'd left their roots and who seemed invigorated thereby. Isabel Allende from Chile to California, Clarice Lispector from Russia to Brazil, Haruki Murakami from Japan to Italy, Kazuo Ishiguro from Japan to England. I knew I wasn't going back to New England, that I'd found my real homeland. North California was where my characters wanted to be.

Rusty came and went irregularly, still busy with family affairs. No sign of Wade. Lia and I lived happily together. She was silent but not brooding. She was always busy and seemed to have infinite inner resources.

Sometimes I took a break and went to sit on the fountain to check out her activities. She was still developing the new pantomime, but it didn't draw a crowd like bashing her head into the lamppost had done. It was a really boring pantomime consisting solely of reaching into her watch pocket for a watch, winding it, and shaking it. The gestures were too minute. Instead, one tended to watch the intentness of her eyes and face, which looked as if she were performing a crucial experiment, Marie Curie discovering radium.

One evening Rusty came by. Lia and I had scrounged

some driftwood from the bayside and built a fairly nice fire. It wasn't a big blaze, but it was colorful with blue and green flames mixed in with the orange and yellow because of something in the wood, probably some spilled pluto- nium. We were stretched out on the floor in front of it, playing checkers at the same speed the Russian grand mas- ters played chess only, unlike them, laughing our heads off whenever we took a man.

Rusty sat down with a beer. His amiable face looked, well, not exactly disgusted, but close, a sort of amiable repugnance.

"What's the matter, honey?"

"This place. Are you waiting for Nancy to get home to clean it up?"

Sheepishly, I sat up and looked around. It looked okay to me. The covers were neatly thrown over the unmade beds. There were some fast-food cartons around, clothes draped on chairs. The dining table was covered with my writing work —a beautiful sight to see. I'd never dared use the table when Nancy was home, spreading out like that with my typewriter, books, and papers there night and day. There were crunkled-up papers littering the floor around the chair, *way* around it. It looked great. On other surfaces were open books. I liked to read about five books at a time and leave them open to my place.

Right then I knew I couldn't room with Nancy any more and worry about whether I held or lost a job and have to pretend I was employed when I wasn't. I knew I wanted my own place no matter how small, no matter how bad a loca- tion in the city, just so that I could leave my writing work out and come and go from it at any hour and not have to adjust to someone sleeping or her wanting to set the table for dinner. Some little hole-in-the-wall in which every nook and cranny belonged to me at all hours of the day and night.

Then I looked at Rusty, who had started this line of thought and I remembered I was going to marry him. Wouldn't it be the same, maybe worse? He'd come home from the firehouse and want the place looking nice. He'd want the table set, a chicken in the oven, the bed made, maybe some decorative effect that wasn't cobwebs.

But to have my own place to write in wasn't enough. I had to live too. I had to take on life, connect with others. Love. Work. Have babies. Make beds. Get down on my knees and scrub. Make compromises. Otherwise my writing would dry up and when someone opened the book I finally got published, sand would fall out instead of juice. My words, instead of causing the blood to pump wildly to the reader's head and heart, would throw dust in his face, make him scrinch up his eyes and snort.

Still, if Rusty was a man to whom it was super important that his home look nice, which is the sort of thing you don't consider when you first throw yourself into a lover's arms (how they like their meat done and if they bounce a coin off the just-made bed for a tautness test) then maybe we weren't so right for each other, maybe living together would be hell on earth.

By now a little while had gone by and I guess both Lia and I were staring at him like he'd killed puppy. He started to blush.

I panicked, jumped to my feet, messing up the game which made Lia cry out, but this time, instead of rushing to Rusty to cover his face with kisses, I ran out of the apartment so I wouldn't have to see the gargoyle.

Outside, I calmed down and was glad I'd come. The night was so pretty, the air so sweet and soft, full of spring. I leaned against the lamppost, *our* lamppost, looking at the Bay, at a freighter moseying out under the bridge to the Orient, all lit up like a party.

Rusty found me a little later. He put his arms around

155

me, his wonderful, big, shapely arms. "Will you sing to me?" he asked.

I sang Bessie Smith's "Nobody Knows You When You're Down and Out." " 'In my pockets not one penny,' " I crooned, " 'And my friends I haven't any . . .' "

There was a woman to whom for sure life was everywhere life. A great artist. I told Rusty about her and how she died bleeding to death because they wouldn't let her into a white hospital.

Then Rusty said good night. It seemed like he'd gone from being a lover to a visitor, gone from admiring me to disapproving of me. Although he still liked my singing. That was good. Probably he just had a lot on his mind.

It wasn't until four days after the funeral that Lia's pantomime began to coalesce for me. By now there was more to it. She'd added some action beyond infinitesimal finger movements. She walked over to a place and fiddled around and then started pouring something into some vessel and handing it to another person. What got my attention was, she walked differently. It was a splendid walk. It proved she could walk well normally if she wanted to, if she thought about it.

Who's walk was this? Wade's. To a T. When she reached into the little watch pocket in her jeans, my hair began to stand on end because I realized that it wasn't a watch she was pulling out. No, *it was a little packet* and she was tearing its top off and pouring whatever was in the packet into a coffee cup. Then she was crinkling it up and sticking it into her hip pocket.

Oh Lord. I felt faint. I felt sick and nauseated. It was just like the screenplay. He'd done it.

But what had he done? Was he just going to play a trick on his mother like in the original script? Or was he trying to poison someone? If so, surely not his mother. His grief

156

was too real, too horrible, he loved her too much. Unless the poison was meant for someone else and it misfired. I tried to remember if all the cups were the same pattern and couldn't.

I staggered back up to the apartment, threw myself down on my unmade bed, falling into a swoon. In a swoon was just where I wanted to be.

When I came to, I tried to think what to do with this information, who to tell and what to tell. If only, oh if *only* I had mentioned the play and my anxieties surrounding it to someone, then . . . then what? Well, then I could go to that person and say . . . what? That it had happened! What happened?

That Wade maybe killed his mother.

And on what do you base this knowledge of him *maybe* killing his mother? Besides the play you told no one about?

This is Your Honor talking now, playing Devil's Advocate. Wouldn't you know he'd turn up? As usual, he's making *me* feel like the miscreant even though I've come to him in all good faith, believing in justice.

I base it on Lia's pantomime, you fucker. (This last was under my breath.) You remember her, m Gromy, from the other cases you've tried about me.

A retarded child, as I remember.

Everyone thinks she is but she's not.

Let's hear what she has to say.

Good idea, Your Honor!

Energized by Your Honor's excellent idea, I raced out of the apartment and nabbed Lia, who was setting off with a crony to the Marina Green for some kite football.

"Lia honey, this pantomime you're doing seems to show Wade opening a packet and putting its contents into a cup. Is that right?"

She just looked at me.

"Speak!" I shouted at her. "Will you please speak, just this once?"

She began to cringe a little and look hunted. I was reminded of the day I saw her mother beleaguering her. Was I, like the accursed note predicted, taking on Mrs. D's hateful role in the family?

Previously I'd never asked anything of Lia. She knew I felt unqualified love for her, accepted and admired her for exactly who she was. Now I was dressing her up, making her go to the funeral, trying to force her to speak, just as her mother must have done countless times.

Except for the one small "m Gromy" she'd uttered when I went to the mansion to bring her here, she'd stopped speaking her own language let alone begun speaking mine. But I still believed in her turnaround at the funeral, felt she was biding her time. Maybe she wasn't speaking because what she had to say was too appalling.

I let her go. I'd sort of desperately seized on to her. I should never have listened to Your Honor.

I said, "I'm sorry," and right away regretted it because it seemed I was starting to perceive her as the others did instead of as a person who knew exactly what she was doing. So I said, "I'm sorry for acting so anxious, but I think if you know something about your mother's death, you should tell me."

She *had* told me in the way she knew how.

"In English," I added.

But she was looking off now, seeming not to hear me.

I spent the rest of the day trying to reach Daddy. When I did, I laid the whole thing out to him from start to finish since I'd previously not told him about the play from hell and it was news to him about Mrs. DeRosa's suicide. Through the muddled description of events, he caught hold of the salient points and, even based though it was on a suspect pantomime, he thought I had cause for alarm.

"What you've got to do," he said, "is go to Wade's cottage sometime when he's not there, when you're *sure* he's not there, and see what else he has written in the script, or put down on tape. I assume you have a key."

"Well, he fired me, but come to think of it, I do still have his key."

"It's telling that he fired you. This way you could not be privy to his further writings. If he has hired someone new, he will have learned to hire someone with no imagination."

"Yes." I smiled. "Thanks, Daddy. I'll keep you posted. I feel much better now that I have something to do."

FOURTEEN

The next night at eight o'clock found me in front of the Hyde Street cottage. I crept up the steep steps to Wade's front door and let myself in with the key.

Lia was home with Nancy, who was back from L.A. Wade and Rusty were having dinner together. I'd asked Rusty to invite him out and admitted that I was making a secret foray to Wade's office but I hadn't said why, wanting to have more information before even hinting anything to Rusty.

A part of me, a big part, was feeling I should leave well enough alone, that this was a crazy family I'd gotten mixed up with and whatever they did or didn't do to one another was none of my business. The woman was dead. If Wade had killed her by mistake, nothing Your Honor could think of would be worse punishment than the grief he was now suffering.

But then there was all the money that should rightfully go to the others. If Wade had murdered her, he shouldn't benefit.

I sidled in the front door, leaving it unlatched behind me for a quick getaway. I realized I should have an alternative exit, so I unlocked and opened the back door as well. It went from the kitchen to a flowerless patio. Wade had done nothing with it, leaving the previous tenant's boxes of flowers to wither and die. One box had long dried grasses and a tipped-over white plaster head of Beethoven that looked ghostly in the dusk. Behind the patio was natural hillside on which some red geraniums grew wild. Back here, I could make a getaway two ways: by scrambling up the hill, or exiting through the gate to the alley which led along the side of the house past garbage cans back to Hyde Street. I took the alley gate off the latch.

Feeling secure now, I returned to the cottage and hied myself to Wade's office. I rummaged about and found the script. There was nothing new on it since I'd typed the last tape, ending with Mrs. D, having been dressed by Lily, going happily into the party. The last line was: "The wife and mother is heartbreakingly beautiful and everyone in the house hates her, especially her special friend."

I searched some more to no avail. It was in his bedroom, in the bedside table drawer, that I found the tape recorder. I wanted to take it and run but I rewound it to listen in situ. It began where it had before. "It is a filthy wet and cold evening in November." I fast-forwarded it to ". . . especially her special friend."

There was silence for a minute before it began anew. But it didn't pick up where it left off at the party. Instead, it began the next morning:

"The next morning Dark got a call that his mother had suicided. His first horrible thought was that he had killed the wrong person. But no. That was impossible. His intended victim never drank the coffee that contained the poison and he was absolutely certain it had not gone to his mother by mistake. Nor could she have returned to the table and drunk it later since, while the others were at their cognac, Dark had dumped it out.

"So it must truly have been a suicide. She'd threatened before, attempted before, written many such notes. This time, by an uncanny chance, she'd pulled it off.

162

"Unless someone at the dinner intended her murder and succeeded.

"Why had the husband not found the body until morning? Had he taken the mistress home and stayed with her?

"Had the mistress finally seen her chance and done the deed herself, tired of waiting for her lover to do something on his own?"

There the tape ended, wait as I might for more, straining my ears to hear for an end part, or better, an elucidating middle.

Never mind his speculations regarding his mother's death. Who was *his* intended victim? The only ones who hadn't drunk their coffee (this I remembered, the only thing I did remember aside from my dragging leg) were Milton and me, and Rusty, who drank half.

His target must have been Milton, mustn't it have?

What if it were me? Why? Why me, the one who was hardly in the play in the first place and in the last place too, being so lacking in vividness?

No, I couldn't claim colorlessness this time. It was my engagement party and not to him.

Was that it? Had I hurt him?

My behavior to him could appear to an outside observer to be abominable.

I had worked on his sympathy in the post office. He had hired me out of the goodness of his heart, although I wasn't what he wanted. We had made love and it had been wonderful. He assumed I was now his girl, maybe his fiancée. The next day he learns I am connected somehow with his missing brother. In a pique I quit on him. I return at the behest of his mother but he soon learns I am engaged to his brother and have come back to work only "for the money."

Men have killed for less shabby treatment; for overcooking their eggs or not darning their socks.

Even if it weren't a wounded heart that prompted it, it

163

could have been his wounded ego. The beautiful, world-famous model scorned by a bland-faced girl who instead chooses his younger brother (who he hated, in the first version of the script, and was jealous of).

Still, it would be pathological. Milton as the intended victim made more sense.

What about Rusty, who'd drunk half a cup and whose strong constitution might have survived a half dose of whatever it was?

My speculations about his victim were going the same place his had over his mother—nowhere. It was all extremely nebulous. And again I had to remind myself it was a play, not a deposition, not even a journal.

However, putting it together with Lia's pantomime, it sure seemed like a packet of something from his pocket went into someone's cup and was drunk, not drunk, or half drunk.

My rummaging, listening, and speculating had taken some time. I decided to head out. It occurred to me I'd left fingerprints. So what? It wasn't a murder scene. But I wouldn't put anything past Wade in detecting someone had been here and subsequently finding out who. I whipped off my shirt and wiped everything I'd touched in the bedroom and was heading for the office, when I heard a key in the lock.

Oh Lord. Maybe it would be a murder scene after all.

I wheeled to run out the back door but then realized the front door wasn't opening. Had I imagined it? A cable car rumbled by, drowning out all other sounds. What if he'd discovered the door was unlocked and decided to go around back to head off the intruder's retreat. I didn't know what to do, what door to leave in a hurry by. I went to the front door and tried it. It was locked. He'd locked it and gone around to the back. So I should unlock it and go out the

164

front. I unlocked it. But I was scared to open it. He could be standing right there. It could be a trick.

I ran like hell through the living room, office, kitchen, out the back door, hearing the gate latch click as he came through it to the patio, and closed it behind.

We practically ran into each other. I screamed and dropped my shirt that I still clutched in my hands from the unfinished fingerprint-wiping job. I turned tail and began scrambling up the slope in back of the patio through the welter of red flowers. He didn't come after me and presently I saw why he didn't need to. The geranium forest was fenced in by one of those unassailable, by me anyhow, hurricane fences.

I ran from one side to the other like a monkey who's just been caged, or a baboon. It occurred to me that I was naked from the waist up and my white breasts loomed in the dark like Beethoven's tipped-over head. I felt they bobbed and beamed blurrily like little signal lights telling him where I was.

Wade called up to me, "Rome! Come down here. You're being a fool. I'm not going to hurt you, for Christ sake. Come on down and put your shirt on. We'll talk."

It seemed like a good idea, but then everyone's ideas had seemed good to me: Your Honor's, Daddy's, Dostoevsky's. Then they turned out to be bad ideas.

I came down. There was no alternative.

We walked into the house, Wade carrying my shirt, and there was Rusty. He was speechless but thank goodness he didn't start to blush. I couldn't have handled it along with the rest of the situation that I couldn't handle. I tried to be cool and used the time-honored remark for such fixes: "Anything to drink around here?"

"No," said Wade, "you drank everything up when you worked for me."

"That's not true!" I exclaimed, losing my cool right off the bat. I grabbed for my shirt. "Give me that."

"I want you to tell me why you are here, but I particularly want to know why you are here with no shirt on."

I was glad it was he who asked so Rusty would understand right away that I hadn't taken my shirt off for Wade. I was double glad Wade was bewildered. It restored my confidence. I pulled my shirt on over my head, not bothering to turn. Let them see. It wasn't as if they both didn't know my bosoms pretty well, hard to say who better.

Rusty spoke hesitatingly. "Rome, when Wade left suddenly I figured I better come along after him, knowing you were here. However I too don't know why you're here and I think you'd better tell us both."

He sounded ever so slightly stern, like the time he'd said I wasn't nice about him standing by Milton, the time he made me feel sheepish (The first time. This was actually the third, the second being when he said the apartment was messy and asked when was I going to clean it).

Seeing my face, he added kindly, "I'm sure Wade has something for you to drink. I'll look." He went to the kitchen and Wade and I stared at each other like kids do to see who can make the other blink first. He was winning, but I pretended it was just Rusty coming back with my drink that made me look away.

He carried a bottle of red and three goblets. We sat down in the living room like civilized people, only when we drank no one said Cheers. They waited for me to explain (and to finish swallowing and pouring another).

"Okay," I began. "You know Lia's new pantomime?"

"Yeah," they both said, "the one about the watch. The boring one."

"I observed it carefully and it wasn't so boring. It shows Wade taking a packet out of his watch pocket, tearing off a corner, shaking its contents into a cup. The reason I recog-

166

nized the gesture was that it happened in a script of Wade's. I came here tonight to look at the script, refresh my memory, perhaps learn more. I was alarmed. It wasn't that I thought he had a hand in his mother's death, just that . . . something else might have happened," I finished lamely. The whole exposition had been completely unpersuasive. "But . . ." I paused. Should I say this? What the hell. "I do think he had a packet at the party."

Rusty was quiet, almost disinterested. Who could blame him? I'd made it sound like a traffic report.

"Maybe I was going to kill Milton," Wade said. "But the only thing that keeps me going these days is knowing that Milton is alive and isn't getting Mom's money and therefore isn't getting Lily either."

I wanted to tell him Lily didn't care about the money, but that was getting off the subject.

"It really is a pantomime about a watch," Rusty said to me gently. "One day Lia saw a man with one of those old watches on a chain that he kept in his watch pocket and she was captivated."

Wade seemed to look at Rusty with surprise. I recollected that in the First Version of the Script, Rusty had protected Wade, taken the cup, dumped it, gone away. Was he protecting Wade now with this mythical old man?

"Don't disappoint Rome. She wants me to be a killer. But if it wasn't Milton, it must have been Rome I tried to bump off."

"Take it easy, Wade," said Rusty. "You're just saying that because you're upset she came here tonight. You know you are morbidly sensitive and imagine people are trying to hurt you."

Wade, sensitive? It was obviously true of Rusty and Lia, but Wade was such a success in life that he seemed the only tough one. Could he be so sensitive he tried to kill people who hurt his feelings by getting engaged to his brother?

167

Pouring a third glass of wine, I decided Rusty and I should leave right away for Chicago. Wade didn't know his address there or mine in New England. I could change my name, not to DeRosa.

I chugged the wine, looked down to see if my shirt was still on, and stood up. "Let's go." I didn't add "to Chicago." I'd wait until we were in the car.

Once in the car, I didn't get to say Let's go to Chicago, because Rusty asked me, "Why did you have your shirt off? Why was Wade carrying it?"

As we drove, I told him exactly how it all happened. It began to sound funny to me, but Rusty didn't laugh, instead said mournfully, "There you were, standing there with no shirt on, no bra, and it didn't seem to matter. Wade even seemed *used* to it."

Here was a good opening to at last tell the truth to Rusty about me and Wade, but I didn't. Instead, I said glibly. "Well, I *am* sort of built like a boy."

"Your breasts are unbelievably beautiful."

I've been to boarding school and college and seen every kind of breast under the sun, and mine were pitiful. As usual, I was thrilled and touched that his perception of me was so off. "Rusty, can I spend the night with you?" By now he'd stopped at the Alhambra.

He got out and came around to open the door for me. "I'm sorry, honey, but I'm staying at Dad's and it would be awkward. I know he's waiting up for me right now."

"How about if we go by your friend's apartment for a little while," I said as we walked by the fountain to the door.

"I do want to be with you, but I'm worried about Dad. He's had these erratic heartbeats."

I was getting the message. Why be turned down three times? Twice would do. He gave me a nice kiss, sort of a kindly kiss, and left me at the door. I watched him depart, feeling sad. We hadn't made love for a long while. I counted. Not since the day of our engagement party. In fact, I'd made love to Wade more recently than Rusty, although it didn't count since we were insensible with grief at the time.

I felt sad and I felt bad too. I wandered back to the fountain and sat down on the cold tiles, hoping to be soothed by the jauntily plashing waters. It was important to have a look at myself in the light of Wade being morbidly sensitive. I had behaved like a brute. It didn't warrant murder on his part, but it certainly warranted some self-examination on mine.

I was deceitful, selfish, inconsiderate. I cared about myself and my writing to the exclusion of others. What was it Nancy said about my going my own way and causing havoc and not caring? It was true.

I felt so bad that for the first time I wished I could talk to Mother and have her blame herself, say it was all her fault for being such a bad mother. But it wasn't her fault, it was mine. I was a heedless, careless rat. Even running off to San Francisco and not telling Daddy was thoughtless and mean. And I'm a horrible roommate too. Nancy said so.

She tells me what's what. So does Wade. Rusty still seems to think I'm wonderful but not enough to sleep with me. Lia doesn't talk to me anymore. As for Your Honor . . .

I tried to make a joke about Your Honor, but it was too late, I was crying.

I should just let Wade go ahead and murder me, I decided. It's what I deserve. But not until I finish my novel.

I began to suspect this was a mock sorrow I was indulging, that I was luxuriating in a pseudo misery so that I could feel I was a deep person instead of the fool that I was. I didn't really believe I was bad or, if I did, I didn't believe having these wretched traits mattered, because people would care for me regardless. Just as a paranoid sees enemies where there are no enemies, I saw friends where there were no friends, love where there was no love, or where it was fading fast.

A shadow seemed to fall but, being night, shadows couldn't. I was aware of a dark presence, something more palpable than my conscience, a man, in fact, standing in front of me. I lifted my bowed head. It was Wade.

FIFTEEN

He sat down and lit a cigarette. I didn't know he smoked them. It was a foul black tobacco, probably a Gauloise. It would be like him to effect a French cigarette when he couldn't put his hands on a Cuban cigar. I personally didn't think enough people would be wowed to make it worth getting lung cancer, but why should I worry about the lungs of a man who wanted to murder me?

"It was a joke," he said, leaning back and blowing smoke.

"What was a joke?"

"I did have a packet in my watch pocket at the party. I poured it into a cup and told Lia to give it to you. I thought you'd see me do it. I thought you'd be watching me like a hawk and it would scare the pants off you."

"I didn't notice. I guess I wasn't watching. I know I meant to."

"You were probably too drunk."

I didn't respond because I was thinking, how did this jibe with what I'd heard on the tape? It didn't jibe, not at all. Was he trying to throw me off the scent? If so, what scent was he throwing me off of?

"What was in this famous packet?" I asked.

"It doesn't matter."

"It matters if it was strychnine."

171

"Why are you sitting here crying?"

"Because I'm so deep in the lacquer bucket."

He laughed a true, full laugh of happy amusement. "That's wonderful," he said. "Is it a black lacquer bucket?"

"How did you know?" I was astonished. I of course had learned about it from Daddy. It seemed marvelous to me that Wade would know an arcane bit of knowledge that Daddy knew.

"I just supposed it was a pit you were in, only being you, it would be a fancy one."

"In Buddhism," I explained, "it's a metaphor for ignorance. The ancients say that if you live a life of no expectations, of dignity as a monk, being virtuous, doing good without getting puffed up about it, then you have broken out of the black lacquer bucket. You'd definitely have to break out. The sides would be too slippery to climb out," I said, showing I'd figured out that much.

He laughed again. "That's right, Rome, you can't make a sneaky getaway from ignorance. And no one can throw you a rope. You have to live right and do right, then you're out."

"I'll never get out, then. I'm caught. I don't even *try* to live right. And my life is one huge vile expectation of becoming a great writer. What about you?"

"After I've become rich and famous, maybe I'll give it all away and be a monk. But probably not. If I did, it would be out of boredom, not goodness."

"You already are rich and famous."

"Yes, like your father."

I sat up alertly. "Why do you say that?"

"Because you're always portraying him as some wise old monk sitting there uttering pearls of wisdom all day long and the man's an international playboy who used to be a fairly good cook."

"How dare you!"

"How dare I what? Tell the truth? If he's such a god, why did your mother commit suicide? Why did run you away from him? Why have you got a drinking problem?"

"The only problem I have with my drinking is not getting enough to drink. Daddy's the best man in the world and loves me very much."

"What's so loving about him cutting you off because you wanted to follow your own path and be a writer. You were half starved when I met you and on top of that—"

"Just shut up, Wade. You're grieving for your mother and you're taking it out on me. Also, you never had a father of your own." (Or, I would have liked to add, a drinking problem of your own.)

I certainly wasn't going to blame Daddy for any of my problems. He'd told me not to.

"Ha!" It was the same kind of laugh his mother used to make.

A strange thing happened. Although we were in the middle of an engrossing exchange, practically a fight, we both stopped talking. It wasn't that we didn't have more to say. We did. Plenty. But we fell silent, as if the other person wasn't there anymore, we were each alone, thinking our own thoughts. Five minutes could have passed or a half hour. We were together and yet we weren't together. We seemed to have heard yet not to have heard. Maybe the laugh had reminded us both of Mrs. D and we were being silent for her. It was a moment of grace, a half hour of grace, a cease-fire, a truce, a laying down of arms, putting aside of ire. Maybe we were forgiving each other.

He stood up and said, "Let's go."

"Where?" I asked suspiciously, because the grace period, or whatever it was, ended as soon as the silence did.

"Let's go see Lily," he said surprisingly.

Well, I always liked to see Lily any time of day or night and I didn't want to go to bed, didn't feel in the least tired

(I was too hurt with Rusty to feel tired), so I said, "Okay, let's."

I tried to get him to walk, but he refused, so we got into his van. He probably drove such an ordinary car to prove he wasn't an international playboy.

"I'd like to get Lily to fill us in on where she and Milton were during the time Mom was dying," he said as we drove to her apartment and around endless blocks to look for a parking space. By the time we walked from the parking space we finally found, we'd have done better to have walked from the fountain, which, naturally, I pointed out to him several times.

As Wade and I approached Lily's apartment, I saw a disturbing sight. I detained Wade, pulling him into the shadows so I could watch. It was Milton, leaving Lily's building, and I never saw a man happier in heart, a man so spritely, walking on the balls of his feet, practically clicking his heels in the air.

This was the man who was waiting for Rusty to get home to be with him, the man who was so emotionally upset and so physically poorly as to be having heart pains, so troubled that I couldn't "count" on going away to Chicago with Rusty because Rusty was so needed by him. This man, ostensibly crushed by twin griefs of losing wife and fortune and with a third grief on the horizon of losing his mistress, looked like a man who'd won the lottery and just had a good fuck besides.

I could feel Wade tremble beside me. "The bastard," he said. "The bastard."

"Wade, let me go in alone. You're too upset and Lily will talk better with just me there."

He agreed.

Once inside, I found that Lily looked pretty smiley herself. She was having a cup of tea and poured me one.

"What brings you here at this hour?" she asked.

"I was feeling down in the dumps. Rusty left me to be with Milton, but I guess Milton was here."

"Yes, he was."

"The guy was dancing out the door. And you look happy too. How come?"

"Well, between us, their lawyer has come forward with the official will and there seems to be no question but that her holograph will, i.e., the suicide note, will be thrown out by virtue of her not being of sound mind. Milton gets the store, and the money will be divided among the four of them."

"I see." I wondered what had happened to her other feelings about Milton vis-à-vis him not leaving Mrs. D, because he was tied to her dough.

"Of course Wade could fight the old will," I said half-heartedly. The whole thing was too depressing for words.

"Yes, he could," she said equably. "But he won't. Sit down, dear." I did. "Wade is something of a practical joker, you know. He was always threatening to put glass in his mother's drinks" (a whole windowpane, I remembered) "so she'd have justification for her maddening fears. I'm afraid he did some joke of that nature that night. Naturally, we want to keep it all in the family. However, if he went to court to fight the will, it would have to come out."

I was silent. There was lots I could say, but I figured better not. Anyhow, I was too depressed for words.

"Milton saw him pour something in her cup. Lia saw too."

My silence became morose. She was still talking but I tuned out. I could say that he'd put it in my cup, not Mrs. D's, but what would that accomplish? It was too much for me and mint tea didn't give me much fortitude. I forced it down and got out of there, mustering up minimal warmth for a good-night hug.

Wade, being a habitual listener behind doors, was waiting in the hall. He took me by the elbow and hustled me out. "I heard," he said. "But it's all trumpery. I played a joke, but it was on you, not Mom. They think they've got me trapped, but they don't. They may be right about the will being no good, but only if it was a suicide. I think it was murder."

We walked along, he kicking out at anything in his path or, if there wasn't anything, running over to kick the side of the building.

"Why did Rusty say that about the watch?" I thought to inquire. "Lia's pantomime being about a watch?"

He didn't answer, instead attacked. "You didn't even ask Lily about the rest of the evening like you were supposed to. If Mom was writing her suicide letter before dinner, which Rusty says she was, then what if Milton saw the letter and decided to help her along with her task."

That supposition had too many holes in it to warrant a reply.

"Christ," he continued expostulating, continued kicking things, "she was always writing suicide letters. He could have used an old one. It was her main form of communication to him. Where are you going?"

"I'm walking home." I veered off at a right angle, sick of the subject, and more sick that Rusty either lied about Milton needing him home tonight or, upon finding him gone, didn't care enough to return to me.

I crept in quietly so as not to disturb Lia and Nancy and curled up in a sleeping bag on the floor. In the morning I awoke wondering how Wade knew my father was a cook. Although during the post office scene, I'd babbled about Daddy cutting me off, I'd never said anything about who he was or what he did.

Later in the day I confronted Wade with this question. He'd asked me to come in and do some office work and I obliged, feeling guilty about my break-in of the night before and wanting things to get back to normal, whatever that was. It had been a week since my firing and things had piled up. He himself didn't appear until just as I was leaving. Later I had a date with Rusty, to whom I'd already expressed my hurt that he'd left me to be with the supposedly ailing Milton, but when finding Milton gone, still hadn't returned to me where, twice denied a loving, I sat glumly at the fountain. He said we'd talk about it tonight.

Poised to leave Wade's cottage as he came in the door, I asked him how he knew about Daddy and he told me that, upon learning he was to inherit the store, he had gone down to the Rose for a look around, including a good snoop through Milton's office. Here he found a report about me from a Boston detective.

I was stunned. I sat down. Wade stood, taking off his outer garments as he talked. It was one of those May days in San Francisco that are freezing cold for no reason. The wind was howling down Hyde Street like it had a plane to catch.

"It's not that unusual. I don't think you understand how rich my family is. Imagine Milton's reasoning. His son asks a girl to marry him his first day out of the hospital, asks the girl who put him in the hospital! He proposes when, for all we know, his brain's not yet intact (if it ever was). And, even more amazing, the girl says yes. It begins to seem like a plot. The girl could be a gold digger. She gets poor old Rusty when he's down and vulnerable. The guy's not too swift when he's up and raring to go, mind you."

I glared. He smiled, knowing I knew it was true.

I had begun to realize Rusty wasn't very smart. It's another thing you don't notice during the first week of passionate embraces. You don't notice or care. I still didn't care.

Wade was watching my thoughts. "Back to our gold

177

digger. She's new in town, thinks Milton. Nobody knows her. Let's find out exactly who she is."

"Lily knew me."

"At that point he didn't remember that he'd met you at Lily's, didn't connect you. Lily didn't know the guy you were seeing in the hospital was Rusty."

"Right. Okay, so I see his point, his concern. What did he find out about me?"

"Bad stuff. You'd been kicked out of three schools, two for being drunk and obstreperous, one for using drugs, hard ones."

"I didn't share needles in case you're worried about AIDS."

"Then"—he ignored me—"because of your good SATs you got into a distinguished college but dropped out after a year and a quarter. That was after your mother's suicide, so probably you were a wreck. God knows I'm a wreck."

Today he didn't seem so much of a wreck. He actually seemed in surprising good humor.

"Yeah, but at least my mother's suicide didn't feature a poison packet."

"There was one packet with plain crystals in it which I poured into your cup, uncovertly, for anyone to see, but especially for you to see. It was a joke. It was a mean joke but I was feeling mean. I *am* mean."

"Why did Lily say it went into your mother's cup."

"They want it to be her cup because they want to legalize the old will and scare me off the new one."

"Are you scared off?"

"Hell, no."

"If there's as much money as you say, why not share it out and then everyone's happy."

"Now you do sound like a gold digger."

"Sure. That's why I ran away from my family, who are so

178

rich they wouldn't deign to *shop* at the Rose, let alone own it."

Though you couldn't tell by Mother's wardrobe, I thought, looking down at my current costume that looked like a large version of a bag you put bank money in to carry to an armored car. On her these things had fit. She'd gone to Paris every spring to make her selections at the couture shows. She'd be the only Bostonian there, most of whom, from the old families, wear hand-me-downs, a tradition I was continuing.

"The report concludes that when you dropped out of college your father cut you off and you were unable to get a job anywhere. You came to San Francisco, lived off Nancy, and began worming your way into the DeRosa family from both ends. Of course, our intrepid investigator didn't learn the compelling fact that you slept with me too."

Curiously, all this did not make me feel sheepish. I was sort of impressed by how bad I was, or how bad I could be made to look if someone set about it in the right spirit.

I was thoughtful, making the inevitable connection between this news and Rusty's withdrawing from me. "I guess Milton told all this to Rusty and that's why he's pulling away."

"Is he?"

"Absolutely. It hurts me that he'd be influenced by his father."

"He adores his father as much as you do yours. And when you look at the facts about you, they're pretty bad." He smiled.

"So I'm a little wild. I'm not evil. I don't have a record of marrying men for their money, only of hating school. Isn't it your contention that Milton himself married for money?"

"That's why he's so suspicious."

I stood up. "I've got to go. Do you want me tomorrow? Does this constitute being rehired? I can use the money."

"I can use the help. Here"—he flung his leather bomber jacket over my shoulders—"it's cold out there. Don't worry about being late for Rusty. He's probably at the police station, which is where I've just come from. I asked them to open an investigation of Mom's death now, not wait for the autopsy results."

Stunned, I sat down again, the jacket falling off my shoulders. "You did? But . . . but aren't you worried for yourself? It will all come out about the packet."

"I'm not worried about the fucking packet. Can't you get it through your head there was nothing in it? Now, listen to me. Do you want to know why Mom couldn't have committed suicide, why she never succeeded in any of her supposed attempts?"

"Yes."

"She was psychologically unable to swallow enough pills to do so. Because of all the glass she imagined in any vessel, she couldn't swallow enough liquid to get them down. Yes, she could drink a cup of coffee sometimes, sip by sip, straining it through her teeth, which is what she did that night. There must have been something in her coffee."

"There was the empty Xanax bottle by her bed."

"Yes, there was. It could have been put there later."

"Did you accuse anyone?"

"I told them about Milton and Lily."

"Oh, poor Lily!" I put his jacket on, feeling cold. "Do you think Milton did it?"

"I don't know, but I'm glad to have it looked into, glad to take the bounce out of his step."

I got up to go. At the door I turned for a last pressing question. "Just tell me one thing. In the play you say the poison misfired. Who was supposed to have gotten it? In the story. Milton?"

He said in his most mellifluous voice, as if quoting from the script, the middle part I hadn't seen, "At that point

180

Dark hated everyone at the table, especially the fiancée, who, momentarily, put Dark's other hatreds in the shade."

I put up the collar of his jacket preparatory to taking on the spring typhoon and said sententiously, "If you are serious about writing a play, you can't change your ideas every day. You must decide what the play is about and stick with it and separate it from your life."

"It is about two brothers, a good brother and a bad, and their fiancée."

SIXTEEN

When I got home, Rusty was sitting by the fountain with Lia. He looked unhappy and his face did not light up to see me, although Lia's did a little. Nor did he jump up to greet me in his usual way, instead only glanced at me, then went back to studying the fountain as if he'd thrown a coin in and was waiting for the wish to come true. He seemed prepared to wait at the fountain for his wish even if it meant years and he was not going to be distracted by something inconsequential like a fiancée happening along. It must have been some wish.

I sat down, saying, "Wade told me about the investigation. I'm so sorry. What a mess it all is."

"Mess," said Lia.

"Lia!" I exclaimed. "Are you talking?"

She shook her head no.

"Wade just wants to torment Dad," Rusty said to the fountain. "He even went so far as to tell the police that Lily is his mistress, which is not true. She's always been a close family friend. She was Mom's very best friend. I love Wade and I respect his grief, but he's just lashing out at everyone."

"He believes your mother was murdered."

"No, he doesn't," Rusty said gloomily. "He's just being a troublemaker."

"What do you think, Lia?" I asked her. She shook her head and looked baffled. "Mess," she said.

"Lia, I'm so happy you've decided to talk. I think you are talking."

She smiled but looked dubious.

"Rusty, let's give Lia her supper and then go out for a little dinner together."

"Dad's coming to take Lia home." He looked at me, *finally,* and saw I was made anxious at this news. "Now that Nancy's back, you haven't room for her," he reminded me.

"But . . ."

"She's just going home. She'll still spend most of her time here. Don't worry. We haven't made any other arrangements."

"Is that okay with you, Lia?"

She nodded.

"Are you still staying with your father?" I asked Rusty to sort of see how the ground lay.

"We'll talk about it," he said.

We talked about it. I fixed a little dinner in the apartment. I didn't have a drink. I was waiting until he said or did something loving, then I was going to celebrate. I lit candles and a small fire and made it all nice. Since Nancy was now home, it was tidy. No sign anywhere of a writer in residence. Even the green walls looked fresher, as if watered.

We talked while we were eating. Or I did. I told him I knew about his father investigating me. I said I understood about it but that it really hurt me that he would withdraw from me because his father didn't approve.

"You knew all that stuff about me, honey. And there's nothing bad there. I was just a disturbed kid," I said as if it were all in the past, as if now I was a well-adjusted adult. It was pitiful that I was defending myself, but the hell with being proud. I didn't want to lose Rusty. I loved him.

"So what if I got kicked out of school. So what if I left

184

college. You know I don't care about money. If I did, I wouldn't have gone against Daddy, right? Milton will come around to liking me, when he sees how happy we are together."

I kept going on with the pitiful defense because nothing I said seemed to lighten Rusty's doleful, down-in-the-mouth countenance. He was back to not looking at me, slumped in his chair, his eyes studying his toes.

"Rusty, you know I didn't try to ensnare you. That's ridiculous. When the lamppost knocked you out, I stood by you until you were better. When you asked me to marry you, I said no. Don't you remember? Tell Milton I said no." This was hard, uphill work. Especially without a drink.

"I don't care if we get married. Let's forget the engagement. But let's be lovers again. I want you. I miss you. Can't we be like we were? Please?"

Now I was on my knees before him, trying to get him to at least meet my eyes. "Rusty, speak!"

He began to blush a little. I prayed it wasn't going to be a full-blown tongue twister, the gargoyle. Was he starting to be the blusher again? Was I fulfilling his mother's prophecy, taking over her role to bring misery to the family? Did she used to get on her knees and beg him for emotional support as I was doing? Probably.

For the first time, I began to sympathize a little with the late Mrs. D. I mean, hell, if you couldn't ask your own kids a simple question without their reacting in some utterly grotesque way . . .

But her questions weren't simple. They were maddening.

I got up, thinking to get away. But no. I would not abandon him in his blush. Nor would I avert my eyes and wait it out as they all used to do.

He covered his face.

I remembered how happy he was when he told me he

didn't blush anymore. Now it had all come back. What a nightmare.

When it was over, he looked white and drained. He went over and threw himself down on my bed. After a while, looking at the ceiling, he said, "Dad thinks you're lovers with Wade."

Boy, that Milton was sure out to get me. What did I ever do to him?

I didn't say anything. Why should I say anything if he wouldn't even look at me when he spoke and when he wouldn't respond to me when I begged him to?

Also, what could I say?

He sat up and looked at me. He looked so miserable, I found myself going over and sitting beside him. He took one of my hands in his. Was this enough of a gesture of affection to constitute a celebration, i.e., a drink?

"Rome," he said sweetly. "Of course I don't care about all that other stuff. But I do care if you were lovers with Wade. I care a lot. Apparently Mother thought so. She was surprised you were engaged to me, not him."

"Did you ask Wade?"

"Yes, I did. I should have asked you first, but it was eating away at me and I had to know. He said no. But the fact is, I don't know whether to believe him. He lies so easily. If it's not true that you were his lover, then you have every right to hate me for distrusting you and for being so cold this last week. It is horrible of me to ask. But I've got to know."

"He was the man I'd made love to once, before I met you," I said, sealing my doom. I seemed to hear the huge seal coming down and stamping the wax on my doom declaration. What would the seal say, something in Latin probably, like one of my boarding school seals, *lux et veritas,* light and truth?

Okay, so I was doomed to be without love, but I had let

in light and truth and isn't that what I keep saying I long
for? Yes, but that was before I knew about love and how
nice it was, before I dreamed of our little laughing-all-the-
time family.

Now I was the one studying my toes, but when I forced
myself to look at Rusty, he looked happy, not crushed. In
fact, he was holding both my hands now, not just one. He
was kissing me. He said, "That Wade is the lowest of the
low."

He stood up, finding the sitting position too cramped to
contain his relief. He spread his arms. "That's just the sort
of thing he'd do. Take a girl's virginity and discard her." He
walked around the room sort of dancing, the way his father
had when he left Lily's last night.

More happy thoughts occurred to him. "And of course
you didn't know we were brothers then." He smiled. "I
wasn't even conscious then. It was before you knew me and
before you loved me. Whoopee!" He actually said whoopee.

He went to the refrigerator for a bottle of wine. Maybe he
too had been waiting to celebrate. "So who cares," he called
merrily from the kitchen. He returned with two brimming,
frosty glasses. "It's awkward. I can certainly see why you
didn't want to say anything." We linked arms and drank
from each other's glass. He looked deep into my eyes as he
had that first day. Deep, deep as if to make up for the
glancing he'd been doing lately, the perfidious, sketchy
looks. But he wasn't seeing. If he was seeing, would he be so
happy?

He continued declaiming, inveighing against Wade, defending me with a happy, relieved outrage. "And then he
turns around and fires you when he hears you're engaged to
me. God. Poor Rome. I'm so sorry. I've been such a jerk.
Will you forgive me? Will you take me back?"

Need he ask? I started flinging off my clothes for all I was
worth. "Oh, Rusty, yes. Love me. Come into me. Love me

now." He did. We sealed it with a kiss. With seventy kisses —my kind of seal. Forget light and truth.

But I wasn't allowed to luxuriate in his arms. Afterward, he bounded up and seized his clothes. "I have to go home and tell Dad. I can't stand to have him think ill of you one more minute."

He dressed in a flash, but then, without thinking, he picked up Wade's leather jacket, the jacket lent to me to keep off the wind while walking home from work. Seeing what he held in his hand, staring at it, he asked, "Isn't this Wade's jacket?"

"Yes."

"Why is it here?"

"I wore it home from the office. You would have noticed had you deigned to look at me, but you hardly glanced my way until a half hour ago."

"But, Rome, you told me he'd fired you."

"He did fire me, but then he asked me to come in today and do some work, so I did. He wasn't there. He arrived as I was leaving and lent me his jacket because it was so cold."

He kept holding the jacket and looking at me like I'd tricked him. All his enthusiasm for setting Milton straight seemed to be diminishing at a hurtling rate of speed.

Somehow Wade giving me his jacket to ward off the cold seemed to deny the fact of his being the evil virginity-taker and subsequent firer-of-the-woman-he'd-defiled.

"I don't know," he said slowly, shaking his head in honest bewilderment. "The last time I saw you, you were with Wade with no shirt on. Now here you have his jacket."

He was still holding the jacket like it was Exhibit A. I wished he'd put it the hell down. "Rusty, I explained about the shirt. It was for wiping fingerprints. When Wade suddenly appeared, I ran off into the geraniums without it." I had a huge desire to giggle. It must be nerves. I covered my mouth with my hand and coughed.

"You stood there before us both, both your lovers, bare-breasted, without shame."

Still covering my mouth and coughing, I managed to say, "What's to be ashamed of? They're just breasts." I pointed to them since I was presently just as bare-breasted as the night under discussion. "I don't sanctify them. I have no modesty about nudity and certainly no shame about it. To me it's no different than a man standing bare-chested. Will you please put the jacket down and forget about it. Be happy. Everything's okay between us now. Tell Milton."

He stood there, holding the jacket as if he no longer knew where he was or what he'd been about to do. It was a sorry sight. What had happened was that the jacket had brought home to him the fact that I had been Wade's lover which, in all his excitement and relief, he'd somehow denied when I first admitted it, as if my admitting it cleared me.

The only thing I could think to do was get the jacket away from him no matter what. What I wanted to do was burn the jacket, throw it on the fire that was still fitfully at work on the last piece of driftwood.

I compromised by leaping from the bed, grabbing it from his hands, throwing it on the floor, and frenziedly stamping on it.

He watched me do it, still in a trance.

"There," I said when I was finished. I hugged him. I kissed him. "All gone," I said. *"Finito.* It's you and me against the world. Shoulder to shoulder. Life is everywhere life. What are you going to tell Milton?"

"That you and Wade weren't lovers."

"Good idea!" I laughed. Not a nervous giggle, a belly laugh, with my bare belly and my unhallowed bare breasts

jiggling away, all of which he began to notice and appreciate now that the jacket was trampled to death.

He came out of his vegetative state, smiled, kissed me,
took off his clothes, and made love to me two more times.
Then he went to tell Milton the news.

SEVENTEEN

Before Rusty left he asked me what I was doing the next day. I said, "Nothing,"—a lie. I figured it would be unpolitic to say I was going to work and so raise the ugly specter of the virginity-taker and jacket-lender. Funny that I should go from pretending I had a job to please Nancy to pretending I didn't have one to reassure Rusty.

Funny and discouraging.

In the morning, however, I didn't hustle off to work but lounged around, bringing Nancy up-to-date on: me and Rusty, the DeRosa family situation including Lia's breakthrough saying of "mess," the investigation of me by Milton, and now the probe into Mrs. D's death.

"What a worm that Milton is!" Nancy exclaimed as she leaned over and vigorously brushed her thick honey-colored hair. "Imagine trying to undermine you and Rusty like that. How much money does the family have anyway?" She sat down and pulled on panty hose. "And if there's so much money, why should Milton worry about Rusty's part of it? How does that jeopardize Milton's money?" On went skirt, blouse, and scarf. She looked like a fashion plate without even consulting the mirror.

"Got me," said I, lounging away and not feeling guilty since I really did have a job and Nancy knew I did since I'd never told her about the week I was fired. She'd been away, so I hadn't had to skulk. Well, except for a day or two.

"I can see worrying if someone was after Lia for her money. She needs protection."

Made me think. "Maybe Rusty does too. There's something so innocent about him. He's like Lia in a lot of ways. I have the feeling they sit at the fountain by the hour together, not saying anything and luxuriating in not having to."

"I think it would be just awful not being able to talk."

"I don't know. Maybe it's nice. Sometimes I think the only important communication between people is nonverbal, the way you look at the person, or don't look. Gestures."

"Then why are you so eager for Lia to talk?" Nancy asked.

"So people will treat her right, I guess."

"There are a lot of people who can talk fine who don't get treated right."

"True. How come you're so smart this morning?"

"I don't know, but I can't stand here being philosophical when the world is hanging on my next art sale."

"Nancy! Are you selling now? You didn't tell me?"

"Well"—she smiled happily—"I haven't sold anything yet."

"You will. You'll be great. Congratulations."

"Thanks. This nonverbal look that I'm giving you in parting means Good-bye, have a good day, and look out for Milton. I have a feeling this is just the beginning of his scheme to crush you."

I poured myself a cup of coffee and got back into bed, propped against the pillows, thinking about Milton. He wasn't at all one's idea of a bad guy. Too boring. He was attractive, pleasant, but completely uninteresting. And yet the children's dysfunctions couldn't all have come from

Mrs. D. There must be some way he added to the family misery. Maybe his tendency to investigate people was chronic. Maybe he never allowed any of them any privacy, was always being an inquisitor. Maybe he used thumb-screws.

That would stop them from talking and maybe cause Mrs. D to start asking her own crazed questions instead of answering his.

But she loved him. And Rusty adores him. Only Wade doesn't like him and I'm not sure he likes anyone.

Which reminded me, I was supposed to go to work. I decided to see if I could untrample Wade's jacket. It was still lying all mushed up on the floor, sort of crouching illy, like an animal that has dragged itself into the underbrush to die.

As I was shaking it out and smoothing the leather with my hands, the buzzer buzzed. I started with fright, thinking it might be Rusty coming to catch me with the jacket in my arms.

It was two strangers, police. They wanted to ask me some questions.

I excused myself to the bathroom, where I got out of Nancy's terry-cloth robe and into Mother's tan linen slacks and meal-colored silk blouse. I rolled up the sleeves and legs and whipped on the bone-colored belt with flats to match. I brushed my hair, which matched my outfit, face, and eyes and was prepared to meet the Law.

They declined coffee. I poured a fresh cup and joined them at the dining table. They told me they wanted to ask some questions about the night of the engagement party.

I adopted an insouciant air. "Ask away."

Then they might want me to come down to the station and make a formal statement.

"Happy to oblige."

Right now they just wanted to see if my responses jibed with the others'.

"Sounds reasonable."

Would I, first of all, just tell about the party as I remembered it?

"You bet."

The officer who was doing the questioning was about thirty-five years old with too much hair, mustache, and aftershave. He had a cast in one eye which I guess was better than having one on his leg. The other guy was small and wiry with the stolidness of a much bigger man. Either that or he had a headache.

I told them about the party. The trouble was, I didn't remember much. I blithely rattled along, embroidering. Every so often he interrupted to ask me some detail, and as these interruptions grew more and more frequent, I lost some of the rattle and all of the blitheness. My insouciant air seeped away. These men were serious.

The crux of it all was after dinner. They passed right over the coffee-serving with stunning disinterest, biding their time until everyone rose from the table to have cognac in the living room, at which point they shifted in their chairs and perked up as if now they were getting to the good stuff.

I told them I wasn't around much after dinner because Rusty and I were the first to leave.

My interrogator pretended to check some notes. "Not the first. I believe Mrs. DeRosa had already gone upstairs, retired for the night?"

"Maybe so. I forget. Seemed like we said good night to everyone. . . ."

"Before you left you had a private talk with Mrs. De-Rosa?"

"Yes, that's right, I did." I was mad at myself for responding with three affirmatives. Made me seem nervous. It was like the time I said *out* three times in one sentence to Wade at my job interview.

"Wasn't that in her bedroom? Didn't you talk with her alone in her bedroom and say good night to her there?"

I thought back. I remember she had me up against a wall but I couldn't remember what wall, where. I was pretty sure we hadn't gone upstairs.

I shook my head. "No, it was downstairs."

"Where downstairs?"

I shrugged. "Somewhere off alone, but I don't remember going upstairs." I looked at my watch. "I'm late for work."

"We're almost finished."

At that, instead of going on, he remained silent for a minute, looking at me. Even the eye with the cast in it made its way to me fairly successfully after searching around the room. I let my mind drift. Let him look. Big deal.

"Miss Morrison, would you like to tell me about the conversation you had with Mrs. DeRosa when you went off alone together?"

"No," I said unhesitatingly. I'd definitely stopped rattling. I was going for the single-word answers now. Since it was about Lily and Milton, my lips were sealed.

He nodded. "Was it about your relationship with her other son? The son you weren't engaged to?"

"No."

"Was she warning you that she was going to tell Rusty about your sexual involvement with her other son, Wade?"

"No."

"Are you involved with him?"

"I work for him."

He nodded, waited, looked at me some more. I didn't let my mind drift. I needed it near me. I hadn't expected anything like those questions, but they were pie compared to his next one.

"You were at one time a heroin user, right?"

195

Now, this information might well have been on the detective's report about me that Milton must have obligingly given this man but it was not On Record. My boarding school had thrown me out and told my folks, but I hadn't gone to jail or even reform school, just to another boarding school.

So I said no. After all, what did that have to do with the price of eggs?

He rose to his feet, saying, "Mrs. DeRosa died of a heroin overdose."

This was absolutely stunning news, but it was nothing to what followed.

"There was no needle found anywhere in her room. We think that you administered the heroin to her. We're taking you down to the station."

I was thunderstruck. My jaw dropped. I clamped it shut for appearances' sake, although it felt good open.

"You have the right to remain silent . . ." His partner reeled off the Miranda. I listened attentively. Then he said, "We're coming back with a warrant to search your apartment."

I flushed. All I could think of was that I couldn't bear anyone to find and read even a line of my novel. "Just let me get my things," I said, and I put the hundred and fifty existing pages bulgingly in my purse, explaining, "Work. In case I have to sit around with nothing to do."

I actually smiled. As long as I had my novel with me, I didn't care what happened or how long it took.

It made me feel free. Free and unafraid. What a good feeling to have on the verge of being arrested. It was real. Unfeigned even to myself. Life is everywhere life! Right, Fyodor? It's only being dead that isn't.

I was innocent. Rusty and Nancy and Lily knew I was and I didn't care what anyone else thought—except Daddy, and he was far away. Thank God.

Even if I went to jail for a while, hadn't I been wishing I had my own place to write, no matter what part of the city? I'd get fed too. And wouldn't have to work. It would be just like being in college, only I wouldn't feel deccitful the whole time. Maybe, once in jail, I'd finally stop feeling like a criminal. What's more, I'd finally get to meet Your Honor in person.

As for poor Mrs. D, somehow it didn't surprise me. It made sense.

But where had the needle gone?

Who knew about Mrs. D's habit, or had she kept it secret from everyone? Did someone know and turn a blind eye? Someone like Milton? There was no doubt in my mind that it was a habit. And the police must know too. The coroner would have found tracks. Maybe somewhere hidden, like behind her knees. Though it probably couldn't be a habit of long duration, since it was still giving her pleasure, wasn't solely a vehicle for stopping her pain. I remembered her saying she'd found something that gave her relief from her devils. The heroin provided a lovely dream of everything being under control, a haven from the glass storms.

I had the right to remain silent and I would about my final conversation with Mrs. D so as to protect Lily as well as myself.

I was not without guilt. Hadn't I said the words that might have killed her by telling her I'd met Milton at Lily's, confirmed her worst fears so that she decided to shoot herself up, up, and away, put out the light forever?

But if so, where was the needle? The spoon and the candle? The heroin stash itself?

Okay, suppose Milton saw the whole setup and didn't want to tarnish the family name by this lowlife suicide. He cleans it up and puts out an empty bottle of Xanax, thinking it, along with the suicide note, would do the trick.

That's the only thing that made sense to me. Why didn't it make sense to the police?

Would Milton really let me take the rap rather than embarrass himself socially?

I was thinking about this in the police car, an unmarked Plymouth, on my way to the Hall of Justice.

Lia was at the fountain when they escorted me from the building. I'd smiled and waved jauntily but didn't fool her for a minute. She ran to the police car as it was pulling away. I kept smiling and waving from the window like a beauty queen in a parade.

My absurd elation at the notion of being arrested rapidly dwindled upon seeing how scared Lia looked. My heart began to pound with fear as I began to feel under constraint. At the Hall of Justice, the elevator to the sixth floor was a cage in itself, a presage of doom. Waving and smiling became history. The ignominious strip search started me kicking and screaming so that they had to drag me from one place to another.

I was allowed my two phone calls but couldn't decide who to ring. This is important, I told myself. Think!

Daddy would be unreachable, and I didn't want him to know of my latest disgrace, one of major proportions. Towering disgrace. I had peaked at age nineteen. For the rest of my life my bad behavior was going to seem like good behavior in comparison and maybe it would be good behavior because I'd be in prison. Maybe it was going to be one long devotion to my craft, an odyssey toward non-Nobelism with no outside interference. Rusty could sit and wait for me spinning away like Penelope, and when I returned, like Odysseus, I would kill all his suitors.

Shows how much Odysseus learned in twenty years of odysseying. Probably just coming home made him forget he'd gotten a handle on compassion and wisdom and he started acting like a baby again. It's important not to go home and meet your original self. Also he wasn't striving toward a nonprize as I would be. He was always after glory and spoils, which are a spur to bad behavior, almost an endorsement. No breaking out of the black lacquer bucket for him.

I couldn't call Dostoevsky; he was dead. I could call Lily but I felt I'd put her in an intolerably awkward position, being the lover of the man of whose wife's murder I was accused and being as well the lover of the man who probably accused me.

Nancy would be at work and just keep saying Oh God! I wanted to call Rusty but I felt I might break down again. Right now I was holding on to myself for all I was worth.

I felt like I did the time I held Rusty's bashed-in head on my lap, when I thought: This could be me, all alone in the world with something unimaginably horrible happening in an instant when life was seeming normal, seeming even pretty good. Now it *was* me. I wished there were blood so people could see how I felt.

I called Wade. I wouldn't allow myself to cry with Wade. Also, he was the one with know-how. Rusty would be at a loss.

"Wade!" I shouted, so happy I'd gotten him and not his machine. "Oh, Wade!"

"What is it, Rome? Where are you?"

"Th-th-they've arrested me." I started to cry. What a joke to think I wouldn't cry with Wade, who was the only person I'd ever let myself cry with in my life, whose T-shirt I sopped at first meeting, with whom I'd cried myself into a completely unsuitable coupling.

"Help me, please. Quick!"

It was three days before I was arraigned, the date set for the preliminary hearing, a lawyer appointed from the public defender's office, and bail set.

199

I could have used the incarceration time to do some serious thinking, but I didn't. Transfixed by the thunderbolt of my arrest, I became stupid. However emotionally trying my upbringing was, I was not from the mean streets. I'd sat in luxury's lap from day one. Silver-Spoon City. And by luxury I include intelligent, cultured, educated people all around me, not junkies, alcoholics, and whores or, if they were, they were educated junkies, alkys, and whores, persons who could recognize a Cézanne at twenty paces and quote Shakespeare who, when they got drunk, did so on imported name brands, laughing, dancing, singing, and fucking for fun, not necessity.

These women couldn't put a complete sentence together. I would never be able to romanticize them into being the salt of the earth like Tolstoy's peasants. Never mind culture, they didn't know honesty or decency. Okay, I don't live in the truth, but I aspire! I aspire! Truth is anathema here. As is loyalty, humor, courage, beauty, and compassion. These people are brain dead and the only ones who aren't, who still show signs of life and sparks of intelligence, do so only from feelings of desperation.

In no time at all I would become one of them. Because I was too young and scared to hold on to my shakily consolidated self. In a matter of weeks I'd kill for a cigarette even though I didn't smoke. In jail I not only wouldn't write, I wouldn't last.

Poor Daddy. These women around me were what he feared his daughter would become if she didn't shape up. He *was* from the mean streets. He knew what life had to offer the ill-equipped.

The prosecuting attorney cited my reputation for running away, but I guess I didn't strike the judge as a dangerous character. He didn't strike me any particular way. I was too busy pretending I wasn't there, which was hard because I was wearing prison garb, a brilliant orange jump suit. I felt like one of those cones they put in the road to make cars detour, only not as important.

Bail was set at two hundred thousand and Wade paid the ten percent. I told him if I jumped bail he could just deduct it from my salary.

When I got home, I was still reverberating from the incarceration and began a world-class crying jag. It lasted almost two days. I slept sometimes and different ones spoon-fed me periodically when they weren't sitting around looking helpless or, in Wade's case, disgusted.

It was Lia who got me started crying. When I arrived home and saw her waiting for me at the fountain, she looked so incredibly happy to see me. I had the feeling she hadn't moved from the spot since they took me away, that she'd been standing there with her hand over her eyes against the glare, waiting. As I stepped out of Wade's van she ran to me, really fast, and hugged me hard. Then she started sobbing. That set me off.

It was Lia who began feeding me with a spoon. Leonard Woolf, Virginia's husband, used to do that for her when she was in a bad way, with the same lovely, gallant patience, sometimes taking an hour or more to try to get her to take one spoonful of nourishment.

One time Wade came in when Lia was holding the tea-spoon to my lips and said, "Why don't we do what they do with prematurely born animals and feed her with an eye dropper."

Rusty, in a terrible state of nerves from all this, stopped pacing back and forth, leapt over to Wade, and struck him down, much as he must have leveled the photographer of yore. Then he went briskly into his gargoyle routine while Wade picked himself up and staggered about, caroming off the walls, pretending he was much worse dazed than he was.

Nancy wrung her hands and cried, "Oh, my God!" running from one man to the other. Meanwhile, Lia's spoon didn't quiver, so intent was she on her job, nor did my tears abate. What a quintet we were.

Then, on the second day, alone with Lia, she thrilled me into stopping weeping by saying, "I talk. I talk now for you. I tell everything."

Astounded, I sat up from my boggy bed and began to wring myself out. I was surprised, not only that speech had come at last, but that it wasn't, as I'd somehow expected, complete. I thought she'd just start talking away like the rest of us, not sound like an Italian immigrant in her first month of learning English.

She lit up at my magical improvement, then put her finger to her lips, "Shh," as the door opened. This was to be a secret between us.

It was Lily. "Hello, darling." She came bearing gifts: wine, fruit, flowers. I lit up even more. I'd forgotten about wine and fruit.

Lia went over to the bay window to look at the nonview and kick the wall monotonously, maddeningly. I could see Lily didn't like it much, but how could I say a negative word to she who had been so loving, so staunch.

Lily bustled about, arranging her offerings and tidying the apartment a little while she was at it.

"Perfect timing," I said. "I just stopped crying. I'm going to jump in the shower. Only be a minute. Will you call Rusty and tell him I've stopped crying? He couldn't stand it, so I've hardly seen him."

"Will do."

When I returned, patting myself dry from shower water this time, not tears, Lia was gone. Lily said, "What a relief to see you up and about. I'd been told you were in a terrible state."

Why hadn't she come sooner then, I wondered.

I cursed myself for the ungenerous thought, then simply

asked her, "But, Lily, where have you been? I never heard from you even when I was in jail. . . ."

"I'm sorry, Rome. It was Milton. He's been so unwell himself" (I remembered his bouncing step when I last saw him) "and it didn't seem, well . . . judicious, to leave his side to go to yours."

It seemed both Lily and Rusty used Milton's come-and-go heart trouble for their own purposes.

I looked at her searchingly. We were sitting on my bed now, with the tray of attractive, untouched sustenance between us. I looked around idly for my teaspoon.

"Rome dear." She reached over and put a hand on my knee. "I've been thinking it all over. Your best way out of this. I think you should plead not being in your right mind. Now, hear me out. You have a record of instability. Your mother was certifiably crazy, so there is a genetic imbalance to vouch for. It's common knowledge you wanted to kill your own mother. Denied that, and thrown up against a similar woman who was determined to destroy your engagement to her son, you, well, simply lost all sense. As you are so young, I'm sure you'd get no more than a year or two in some nice sanatarium. Please consider this. It will save your life."

I looked at her wonderingly, hardly believing my ears. Was it because she loved me and was genuinely afraid for me? Did she sincerely think this was helpful advice? Even if predicated on not believing me innocent, was it helpful? Was it based on the detective's report which Milton must be showing around to all and sundry, probably even posting it on Laundromat bulletin-boards? No, the report didn't say I wanted to kill my mother, that was Lily's own contribution.

I said nothing, only avidly commenced eating fruit, swallowing wine, as if there were no tomorrow.

Then, out of the blue, I had my fabulous epiphany.

Illumination.

Samsara.

I broke out of the black lacquer bucket.

"Rome, what is it?" Lily looked alarmed.

"There's no tomorrow," I said with a little smile like Buddha's and Mona Lisa's. "That's it. I understand everything now. There's no tomorrow."

"I'm afraid there assuredly is a tomorrow, Rome, and you are going to have to prepare your defense."

"No, really, everything's all right, believe me."

EIGHTEEN

Lily was right. There was a tomorrow the very next day. By then my samsara was fading although there were still shreds of understanding clinging like tenacious ephemera, sort of a *memory* of having seen the light. This I felt I would always have, even if I no longer had a firm grasp of what the light illuminated.

I gave up trying to explain it to my friends. It didn't translate. Nor did it help that there was a dopey old love song by that name, one of the few I didn't sing to Rusty when he was comatose: "So kiss me, and hold me tight. There's no tomorrow, there's just tonight."

Also, when you break out of the black lacquer bucket you're not supposed to feel all happy and puffed up. You're just supposed to say "ah, so," or something like that, and then shut up about it. As soon as I said to Lily, "I understand everything," I vaulted to the top of the bucket and started the slippery slide back down in. Damn!

Anyhow, no one wanted to talk about esoteric matters. The idea was to get me out of my jam. But if everyone had ideas like Lily's . . .

"Lily thinks I did it," I told Rusty and Wade. "Can you believe that? It's heartbreaking. I feel like she doesn't really know me at all, that she too is going by the detective's report."

We were at Wade's. It was pouring rain, which it wasn't ever supposed to do in late May, although as far as I could tell, San Francisco weather made a habit of being unexpected, unseasonal, and extreme.

We'd met at Wade's for a conference about my case. We were in the living room with bowls, not cups, of coffee, another French pretension of Wade's. The rain drummed on the roof, periodically complimented by the bass viol sound of the passing cable cars. All we needed was someone on keyboard.

I'd been telling them about my illumination until Wade started humming the song, "There's No Tomorrow." I hoped Rusty would knock him flat again (shows how illuminated I was, me and Odysseus) but Rusty just laughed. Then he said, "We really have to talk about your case, Rome." So I said about Lily thinking I'd done it.

"Everybody thinks you did it," Wade said, and he wasn't kidding.

"Rusty, surely you don't!"

"I do, Rome. I don't think you meant to kill her, just to make her feel better. Your idea of kindhearted. That's why you took all the implements away with you. So no one would know. But it backfired."

"You think I carried heroin to our engagement party to shoot your mother up! Come on! Your mother has been on the stuff for months. Maybe a year."

"It's the only thing that makes sense, and I think that's the story you should tell," Rusty insisted.

I told them what I thought was the only thing that made sense, the scenario with Milton—him keeping her habit hush-hush to save family face, him arranging the setup with the Xanax bottle. I was astonished when neither of them could see it. Not even Wade.

"Dad would never let you go to jail if he knew for a fact she'd overdosed herself," Rusty said emphatically.

"He's right," Wade agreed. "It would be completely out of character."

"But he's been trying to crush me. Look at him having me investigated . . . !" I was speechless with surprise at the lack of enthusiasm for my scenario, especially from the Milton-hater himself, who went on to say:

"That was in character. He loves Rusty and thought you were out to take advantage of him. If it had been me, he'd have thought, hooray, let her take him for all he's worth."

"And it is you," Rusty said mournfully. "I know it's you Rome really loves. It's you she called for help."

"But, Rusty . . ."

"Also, Rome, I told Wade we absolutely had to level with each other and he revealed the fact that . . . that . . . you'd made love to each other the day after our engagement party. It's what I mean by saying you have your own ideas of kindheartedness. I know you were just trying to give comfort. That's why I think you gave Mom the heroin, trying to help her in the same spirit you helped Wade but really destroying her. You're a creature of impulse. You don't think, you just feel."

All this was very hard. I felt another crying jag coming on but clamped down. "Wade?" I beseeched him. "What do you think? You must have some explanation. I didn't do it. I didn't. It's intolerable to me that you all should think I did, Lily and Rusty, people I love . . ." I gulped. I clamped.

"I don't think you did it," Wade said. "But the damning thing is that the entry place of the needle is a place Mom couldn't possibly reach on her own, so someone did it." He looked at Rusty. "I know Rome never went upstairs."

I seized on this. "And there's no way I could have given it to her downstairs. We're not talking about a snort of cocaine here. But, Wade, how do you know I never went up to her room?"

"Your leg was dragging too badly. You couldn't lift it. Stairs would be out of the question."

This was a wonderful leg. It got me to meet Rusty. Now it was going to get me out of a murder rap. Repressed hysteria is a wonderful thing.

"The prosecutor's case is crumbling," I told Rusty happily on our way back to the Alhambra. The rain was falling so hard I felt we were driving through a car wash. "Who would ever have thought that benighted dragging leg would be the saving of me? Well, why not? It's a magic leg. It's what made you turn to look at me. We'd never have met were it not for that leg."

I noticed that Rusty did not respond, was perhaps wishing we hadn't met. I felt hurt, a pain in my heart. But I didn't want to get into the business of my misguided kindheartedness. "Do you think the leg will be enough to get me off the hook, Rusty?" I quavered.

"No," he said. "I think it will be easy for them to say you can turn it on and off at will. The dragging, I mean."

"But why would I do that? Why would any young girl want to have a dragging leg?"

"God knows," Rusty sighed. "Why do you do any of the things you do, Rome?"

Right then, by his detached tone more than his words, I knew he didn't love me anymore, that it was all over between us. I was more than he could take, had done more than he could forgive. I was not an easy person to love.

He stopped in front of my building and we sat in the car under the deluge, quiet and contemplative, like those martial artists who stand under waterfalls, only without car roofs taking the brunt of the water.

Lia wouldn't be at the fountain to greet me in this kind of weather. Maybe she'd be in the foyer ripping up magazines.

She loved me.

Lily loved me too.

I could tell Daddy I'd go back to college, then he'd love me.

I'd go back after I was out of jail, that is.

If I got out.

I decided to do the decent thing, show that I could be a class act when the chips were down.

"I release you from our engagement, Rusty. I do love you. You're the most wonderful person I've ever known. With you I've known love and happiness for the first time in my life and I'll never forget it."

I wouldn't. I'd always have the memory of our happiness, just as I would have the shadowy recollection of the illumination. Two fabulous memories to go on with. I was a lucky person. And if tomorrow I'd have no Rusty, no love, that was okay, because there was no tomorrow.

"Thank you, Rome," Rusty said. I could hear the relief in his voice. And the gratitude. It was heartbreaking. Already the memory that would stand me in such good stead was corroded from his being so happy to get rid of me.

Nancy was home. I'd forgotten it was Sunday. I'd forgotten that she loved me too. I poured out my heart, told her it was all over with Rusty.

She listened sorrowfully. She was so wonderful the way she could listen, giving her whole attention and all of her feeling. We'd known each other since we were little girls and had no breasts. I still hardly had any. At the end of a day together, we used to walk each other home from our houses, back and forth, back and forth, finally parting halfway between. Now here we were all grown up in a faraway city and she was sailing along in her life and I was accused of murder, with a broken engagement for topping.

"I'm really sorry, Rome," she said when I was through.

"But, you know, I think Wade's the one you're really in love with."

"Rusty does too, but why? Why do you think that? We don't love each other at all. We barely like each other."

"You're much more yourself with Wade and Rusty says Wade's nicer with you than he's ever been with anyone. Rusty says—"

"Wait a minute. When did Rusty do all this saying?"

"Well, we were together constantly when you were in jail, both of us being so upset."

"Hmmnnn."

There was an awkward silence. I waited for Nancy to say it's not what you think, but she said it was.

"It's what you think," she said. "I'm crazy about him. He's such a wonderful, genuine person compared to all these horrible, brittle, spoiled, superficial men I've met in this town and every other town too."

"Oh, Nancy," I moaned.

"He doesn't know my feelings, Rome. Nothing happened. And nothing ever will either. He'll go back to Chicago and probably take about a year to get over you and that will be that." She jumped up with forced cheeriness. "Let's go to a movie. Let's get our mind off things. It's Sunday."

We went to a movie but my mind didn't. It stayed turning things over like it was going through a chest in the attic. What I kept thinking about, what I kept returning to in my mind again and again was Wade's play. It must contain some clue to the answer, if not the answer itself.

It was a jumble. He was always in the creative process, exploring how he wanted to tell his story, trying to discover what the story ultimately was to be. By writing it, he was trying to work out the relationships within the family, especially that of the two brothers. But the parents' relationship kept getting in the way because of the intense triangle that existed with the mother's special friend. Then there came

210

the triangle with the young girl, me, and the two brothers. From one day to the next he was never sure who, if anyone, was going to be murdered. He tried this and that. If this one, who would the murderer be? If that one, who? This was his way of trying to figure out his life. In all his writing and rewriting (or recording) there was only one constant, one person who was consistently the bad guy, and that was Lily—which was totally unacceptable to me for, even though she didn't believe in me, I still did in her.

The next morning was sunny and Lia was at the fountain when I went out looking for her. We were alone and sat together on the bench, talking. In her Italian-immigrant English she tended to stay in the present tense, so it took me a while to realize that when she said "Lily does it," she meant Lily did it.

I was chilled to the bone. "How do you know?"

"I know."

"Did you see her give your mother the shot?"

"No."

"But she did go upstairs?"

Nodding yes. Then, "She does it more."

I thought about what she meant. "You mean, she'd given your mother shots before?"

"Yuh."

"Good Lord."

"Lie down," Lia said. (It sounded like "Liya downa.")

"Why?"

"Lie down," she insisted. "Over," she said when I lay on my back. I rolled over. She jabbed me on the back of the thigh. "There," she said.

I stayed on my stomach, chin on hands, wondering how to proceed with this information. I felt my mind wanting to blank it out, not credit it. I was growing stupid again. My leg was all right these days, but I was definitely developing

211

a dragging brain. Especially when it came to having to think the unthinkable.

So I blanked. The sun felt so good. I hadn't really been outside for six days. The air was so clear from the rain that the light seemed to ricochet off the buildings and trees.

Lia began to go through a perplexing pantomime I could make nothing of, nor was I going to try. I semi-swooned in the sun. Finally my body, if not my mind, took the decision to go directly to Lily and hear her story.

I hated to leave Lia to an audienceless act. I watched for a minute. It seemed sort of florid and Shakespearean with much weeping and rending of clothes. It looked like a scene between me and my mother. It looked like how my engagement-breaking scene should have gone instead of in the cold, heartless, formal way it had, in the ladylike way Lily would have approved of, Lily, who I'd always wanted for my real mother, who I'd loved instead.

It was not yet nine o'clock. She would be just getting up, having her tea, reading the paper. I decided to go over without calling first. I walked, starting out briskly, then going slower and slower, finally stopping. The truth was, I didn't want to see her. Ever again.

This was my lowest moment. Of all the low moments, this was the worst, worse than the strip search, worse than Rusty lighting up and saying thank you when I let him out of my life.

I was standing sagged against some old, multicolored Victorian for I don't know how long when Lily found me. She was dressed in a red jogging suit, something I didn't know she did, jog, along with her other vigorous acts of: drug trafficking, slaughter, and setting up old friends for murder one.

"Rome, are you all right? Are you coming to see me? Let me help you. Take my arm."

"I know everything, Lily."

"Yes, yes, dear, I know. There's no tomorrow. You told me at the time." She laughed lightly. "Come on in and have some tea." She kept laughing.

Off to a bad start. She was deep in a misunderstanding about the everything I now knew. It had become, for her, a source of amusement. I could follow up with a clarifying statement along the lines of "You did it," but I began to be afraid I'd say, as Lia would, "You do it," and then there would be more laughter, the light, silken laughter of sophisticated amusement at the expense of a crazy girl, genetically vouched for.

The next thing I knew I was at the kitchen table with a cup of tea and everything was as bright and clean and cheery as ever. The tree beyond the window boasted new pinkish-green apples the size of Ping-Pong balls.

Lily had to go to her bedroom to change. When she reappeared, in slacks and a crisp white shirt, I said in a dry, dull voice, "You gave her the overdose. Lia says it isn't the first time you gave her the shot. Was that the reason for your daily visits?"

"Yes," she said. Her face hardly changed. Her body, leaning against the counter, seemed to relax. But when she spoke, her voice was different: older, quavering slightly.

"She told me it was vitamins." Lily now turned and busied herself pouring tea. "Because she was unable to eat very much, the doctor said she should have vitamin shots. She was queasy about giving herself the needle and asked me to do it."

"You believed her?"

"Yes, I did. At first. But she was so concerned that no one else know, and that I take the needle away with me each time, lest someone find it while she was sleeping, I began to suspect it was something else. When she told me it was heroin, she was too addicted to stop and I was in too deep to

213

refuse to help her." She took a sip from her cup and it clattered as she replaced it on the saucer.

She wiped her mouth with a napkin which remained clutched in her hand. "She always prepared the shot herself. That night, of course, the shot was postponed because of the party. This was why she no longer liked parties. When I met her upstairs after dinner, she told me to leave the needle this time but the meaning didn't sink in."

She paused and said parenthetically, "If only I'd understood . . . that this was meant to be the last one."

She sighed and took another sip, again patted her lips as if they were soaked. "She was usually asleep by the time I tidied up and left. This time she was dead.

"When I got home I saw that I had automatically put the needle in my purse as usual."

"But why didn't you just tell the police? It really was a suicide. You were only being a friend."

"And have Milton find out what I'd been doing? Have the whole world find out that I was assisting my lover's wife in her heroin addiction!" She laughed, harshly this time— the silk had shredded. "It doesn't look very good."

"But, Lily, who cares how things look? Wouldn't that be better than . . . than my being blamed, going to court, maybe prison."

"You'll get off, Rome. Anyhow, you're young. You have all your life ahead of you. And I have only a few years left of happiness. I love Milton. I've loved him for so long and finally we can be together."

She didn't love him so much when she thought Wade was going to inherit and Milton would be out on the streets, I remembered. But what did that matter now? That was nothing compared to her trashing my life so as not to look bad in the eyes of the world.

She put on a pale-pink linen blazer that matched her slacks and a small, devilishly cute pink hat. I had on a gray silk T-shirt and Wade's faded jeans I'd worn away from our "insensible-at-the-time" lovemaking.

"I have to go out now."

Out? Did she think her life was just going to go merrily on? "Lily, who put out the Xanax bottle?"

"I did. She was supposed to take it for her obsessive-compulsive syndrome, but she never did."

"And the note?"

"The note was already there."

"Let's go to the police together and tell them the story."

"I'd rather die."

"Then die. And I'll tell the story."

"They're not going to believe you, Rome. And they're certainly not going to believe Lia, even if she could put it into words."

This woman had a heart of iron. And I, who believed myself a master of insight, had had no clue. Well, I'd really known her only as a child, and then, when I came to San Francisco, just took her on trust. Even when she'd said and done things that distressed me, I blocked them out of my mind because she was wonderful Lily.

I had to get tough. "Maybe Milton will believe us. I bet he will."

"I forbid you to upset Milton. He's not very well."

"What right have you to forbid me anything at this point? Who cares about Milton? I suppose he's had another bogus heart attack."

She opened the door and gestured me out. "You can't see him. He's in the hospital this moment, having his heart monitored. He had what seemed like a small attack two nights ago."

We stepped out. She locked the door.

"You've always been like a mother to me," I said sadly.

"Really?"

"Why, yes. Didn't you know?"

215

"I've always been very fond of your whole family, just as I am of the DeRosas. . . ."

"You mean I imagined your being a mother figure? You never once thought of yourself that way?"

"I can see why you would want and need a fantasy mother, and I'm delighted to be selected but, I assure you, a mother I am not! Nor did I ever want to be one."

I was tempted to ask her if she loved me, if she ever had, but I couldn't bring myself to seem to beseech, and anyhow, what did it take to make me see the light? This was a woman who went after what she wanted, trampling everyone in her path.

Then she said, as if answering the unasked, "You are quite a girl, Rome, believe me. I've always admired your spirit, your unconventionality, deplorable though its results sometimes are. It is your mother's spirit. She was a fabulous woman, one of a kind, before she got so sick." She paused and added, enviously it seemed to me, "She was never careful."

I spoke woman to woman, since the mother-daughter scenario had gone out the window. "Look, Lily, just tell the police you thought it was vitamins. They'll understand. Everyone will."

"I'm sorry, it's out of the question."

NINETEEN

There was a message on the machine from Daddy. It was not his custom to call me. It was always I who called him. This could mean only that he had heard the dire news that his daughter was charged with murder.

The message said I was to call him, collect as usual, in Perugia, Italy.

I bit the bullet and punched the numbers.

But no, the news had not yet reached Perugia with its clarion call. Instead, he had his own information to impart. "I've had your young man investigated," he said. "I don't think he's a good bet. He didn't go to college at all, has never worked, and doesn't now. His mother has left all her money to the other son, Wade. My impression is that the two of you would be a hopeless couple. On top of all this, he has a violent streak. He beat up a photographer and left him for dead in the street. This I can't brook, Rome. I can't let you marry a man who might hit you. Hello? Are you there?"

"His father had *me* investigated," I said.

"This is an outrage!"

"He discovered I'm a *really* bad bet, being as I'm a college dropout, a drug fiend, unemployable by anyone except his other son, cut off by my father who, get this, is a playboy and has-been cook."

Daddy laughed heartily. "I'd say that describes the two of us pretty well."

My face made a smile. The first one in a couple of weeks, maybe years. It felt odd. I touched my lips. Yes, they really were smiling. Too bad Nancy couldn't see.

I suddenly wanted to tell Daddy about my illumination, but why wreck it up even more by trying to shout it over the phone. Someday I'd tell him. When we were smoking cigars over that beastly Marc de Bourgogne of his. And he'd acknowledge it. He'd say Ah so, and it would be like him putting a sword on my head and knighting me (although normally if you've been enlightened you don't need to be knighted too).

"How's the food in Perugia?" I asked.

"Sublime. They don't use tomato sauce up here, you know. The cuisine is much more subtle. . . ."

I listened for a while, steeling myself to spill the beans. After all, he was going to hear it soon enough from someone, might as well be me. So I interrupted his intricate tales of succulent sauces and told him everything about Mrs. D's death and my subsequent arrest. It took about ten minutes, maybe more. He listened. He stayed silent except for sometimes making a little grunting sound.

The only thing I didn't tell him about was my dragging leg. I don't know why, but having a dragging leg seemed a worse thing for my father to know about than my being a murder suspect.

Then I finished and waited and he said, "This is some pickle you're in, Rome. You have really outdone yourself this time. I'm practically speechless."

Well, what did I expect, that he'd promise to be on the next plane? Yes. That's what I expected. I still had this idea I was Daddy's little darling. But no. It was over between us when he cut me off, when he didn't believe I could be a writer, only all this time I hadn't really faced up to it.

The moment I held Rusty's bloody head in my lap and realized how alone I was in the world, that was the true enlightenment had I but known it. You're born, you live, you die, and although you want to cling to people for all you're worth, you're on your own the whole time. The great thing about sex is you actually do attach to someone and, for a few blinding minutes, you escape from solitude . . . and, of course, when you're writing you're attached to the universe, but well, when you're accused of murder, suddenly there's no one home. It's sayonara time for friends, fiancés, mother figures, and fathers. You're right, Bessie, nobody knows you when you're down and out.

What I should do is gracefully release Daddy from his fatherhood just as I had Rusty from his engagement, give Daddy his cigar bands back.

"Rome? Are you there? You know I'll do everything I can . . ." His voice sounded weary. He might as well have added the implied, "as usual."

Except be with me, I thought bitterly, because you've got important eating to do all over Europe, with and without tomato sauce.

"As usual," he added, then sighed. "Well, what else does a man have lawyers for?" He laughed. "Come on, stop feeling sorry for yourself. You're the one who wanted to be on your own, don't forget. Talk to me. Tell me what you're going to do."

"Kill Lily."

"Good idea." He laughed again. "Actually, Lily's the one who's really in a jam. I know she'll think better of it and tell the police. She's panicking. As for you, I'd tell Wade and see what he thinks. He's the only one who's on your side. Even Nancy isn't entirely, now that she loves Rusty. You see what love has done to poor Lily. She's lost all reason. Maybe I should talk to her. You call Wade and I'll call Lily."

I threw myself down on my unmade bed to figure out how to proceed and fell into the sweet nepenthe of sleep.

"God, you look awful. I can't believe I ever wanted to make love to you."

It was Wade, sitting there in the green armchair nice as you please. The clock on the mantel told me I'd slept two hours. It was afternoon. He was wearing the same faded jeans I had on and, strangely, a similar gray T-shirt.

"How did you get in?"

"I had keys made. Mind you, you still have a key to my house. It seemed only fair. I've come to take you to lunch. If your leg isn't dragging and if you can eat by yourself. I'm not going to feed you in public. They'll be no teaspoon action."

"Why don't we walk over to the beach and grab a hot dog from the little kiosk."

"Sounds repulsive. Let's go."

We got our hot dogs, bags of chips, Calistoga waters, then threaded through the sunbathers on the grass to the little beach by the St. Francis yacht club. A freighter, although loaded to the gills with containers, slipped out through the Golden Gate like a swan.

The rest of the Bay was abob with fishing boats, ferry boats, sailboats, and a forlorn tug looking for a ship to shove around. Everything gleamed and glittered from the rain. It was so clear you could've seen Japan if Hawaii wasn't in the way and if the earth didn't curve.

I told him about Lily.

He was lying on his back in the sun, having removed his shirt. His dark skin was getting darker by the minute. It was like seeing a photograph develop. I was sitting up, making sand mounds as carefully as if they were going to be judged in a contest.

He was silent, like Daddy had been when I told him,

only he didn't grunt. When I finished, he remained quiet. He lay on his back with his eyes closed, still as stone. I was reminded of Rusty, and it made my heart lurch.

Finally, he said, "Do we believe her? Mightn't she still have premeditatedly murdered Mom, alone or in cahoots with Milton?"

"No. I'm sure it was as she said. But don't you think it's vile that she won't confess, that she's still willing for me to take the rap?"

"It's bad, but not as bad as the deed itself."

It seemed to me worse. It was eating me up.

I drank down the bottle of water, wishing it were rum. I hadn't had a rum since before jail. I hadn't worked on my novel either. When they returned my "personal articles" to me upon my release, my novel lay there like a stack of debris, seeming not to have anything to do with me anymore. I almost didn't take it home. Probably I would trash it and start another.

"Don't you think that was low, Wade? This is the woman I loved like a mother? And I never said one word to the police about her and Milton because of wanting to protect her."

Fog suddenly appeared at the top of the headlands across the Bay and began swooping down this side like Indians in old cowboy movies. The fog looming up over the hills on this sparkling bright day was like the warring Indians silhouetting themselves against the skyline then brimming over the landscape just when the wagon train had accomplished its circle, pastured the horses, and got happy around the chuck wagon. It made me feel all hell was about to break loose.

Wade was saying, "If it were really like she said, why won't she tell the police?"

"If only she would. As it is, there's only Lia to witness, and she's not going to make a good impression. When she

221

had her own language she was mystifyingly impressive, but now . . ."

"It beats me where she got that Italian accent," Wade agreed.

I dug around in the sand some more. "Still, I wish you were right. I'd much rather Lily wanted me to take the rap to save her neck than her name."

It's true. My own gripe against Lily loomed much larger in my mind than the original deed that had wiped Wade's mother off the face of the earth. It was because I didn't see her guilty of anything except her treatment of me. Even she, seeing herself through the eyes of the "world," condemned herself more than I did. It was possible to perceive her helping Mrs. D get her fix as a kindness, although, of course, it wasn't. She was helping her to kill herself by stages.

As soon as she knew it was heroin, Lily should have told Milton and hied Mrs. D to a recovery center. I'd tried the stuff for kicks and scorned it, maybe not being in enough pain to appreciate its stupendous powers of forgetfulness, and wanting my mind at my fingertips, but Mrs. D had definitely embraced the stuff for the rest of the journey. All the way to the River Styx.

I drew a big breath, then said, "I have a confession, Wade. I told Rusty but not you. I really am guilty, moreso than Lily because . . . after dinner, just before she died, I told your mother I'd met Milton one day at Lily's. She asked me and I waffled and then I told her."

Wade brightened. He sat up, kicking apart my prize-winning mounds. "Well, there you are. Motive. Mom probably confronted Lily with this massive betrayal, and Lily gave her the overdose. It was probably all a lie about Mom preparing the dose. Sounds too slick to me. Probably Lily did it each time."

He jumped to his feet, pulled on his shirt. But I wasn't

following. I had plunged back into my personal gripe against Lily, reabsorbed myself in my own dilemma.

I grabbed his knees. "She's my only hope. Please think how to get her to confess."

"I can't believe you're hugging my knees in front of all these people."

"Why are you undoing your pants in front of everyone?" I asked, alarmed, releasing my grip somewhat.

"Don't get excited. I'm just tucking in my shirt."

I suddenly realized this could be the scene Lia had been pantomiming this morning. Now she was clairvoyant.

As we left the beach I saw the fog had streamed down the hills and was surging across the water, but no one else was leaving the beach as if positive it would not make it to the sand and take away their sun. Sure enough, it seemed to be making a left turn, heading for Alcatraz and points east. I wondered how it would have been if the wagon trainers had ignored the plummeting Indians and just gone on with their chores. Would the Red Men have turned left?

Walking back to the apartment, Wade said shakily, "I miss Mom so much. She was a terrible woman. She drove me nuts, but in a way she was so interesting, so alive. I can't explain it exactly. Maybe it's that I felt more alive when I was with her. Involved with her and with life."

"Yes, I see what you mean," I said dolefully, not really seeing.

"In a way, it's how I feel with you."

Oh, great! I quoted, " 'With Rome in the family I leave a worthy successor, one who will cause misery to you all!' "

Wade turned startled eyes on me. "That's from the note."

"Yes."

"But I didn't mean that you made me miserable. That's not what I was saying. I was saying that you make me care about life. Maybe because you care about it so much your-self."

223

"But if you think your mother really cared about life, why did she want to die?"

"That's my whole point. I don't think she did. Wretched though she was—and it all was going to get much worse with the heroin—she wasn't a quitter."

"I don't know, Wade. My mother was a lot like yours. When you're crazy, the day finally comes when life is too painful to go on with. You've burned out everyone who loves you and you feel that they and you would be better off. Your mother told me that if Milton was in love with Lily, she'd just as soon be dead because everyone else hated her except you and she knew you were at your wit's end."

But Wade, unhearing, switched back to Lily. "Can you imagine sleeping with your best friend's husband and giving her heroin to keep her quiet and out of the way?"

"It's all how you look at it. I can easily imagine Milton wanting some sane and happy love, Lily responding, then being unable to stop shooting up your mother, even knowing it was wrong. If it happened like Lily said with the vitamins, I can understand that too. What I can't understand and can hardly believe is her letting me go to jail, knowing the truth." I couldn't help harping on this, her worst crime.

"I can understand it because it's in character with all her other behavior. You idolized her and never saw her real self."

"What am I going to do?"

"Begin by going to the police and telling them everything you know, starting with your last conversation with Mom."

We went to the police station together, but the lieutenant had his own news to greet us with.

"Well, Miss Morrison, your friend Lily has been in here and given us a written statement in a pathetic attempt to try and take the rap for you. She said Mrs. DeRosa asked her to give her this shot of vitamins, so she did. But obviously if it were really true, she would have told me six days ago, when we booked you. Took her that long to think it up."

"It is true," Wade said roughly. "The woman's been my father's mistress for years." He rapped out our version. "She wanted my mother out of the way and she got her out, knowingly or unknowingly. Also, it wasn't the first time she gave her a shot. My sister's seen her do it before. Now that we found her out, she beat us down here to give it her own twist."

He said nothing, only looked us over with his good eye and his bad. I saw us through his eyes—dressed like twins in our pale blue jeans and gray jerseys, Wade with sand in his ears. I imagined how disarming Lily would have been in her immaculate attire, charming ways, Milton not standing beside her in a giveaway identical outfit.

"Now, let's see, Mr. DeRosa, let me get things straight here. You're the accused's lover, is that right?"

"Oh, for Christ's sake. Rome Morrison is engaged to my brother."

"Is that so? I heard the engagement's off now that he found out the truth about you two."

"You heard wrong?"

"No, he's right, Wade. It's all over. But not because of that. Because"—I thought fast—"he didn't believe in me. He thought I'd done it." I took a moment to feel glad that Daddy, at least, had believed in my innocence. It never entered his mind I'd done it. Maybe I *was* his darling girl.

Wade turned and walked off. "Don't bother trying to talk to this clown," he said.

I bothered. Again the vision of Lily in her adorable pink hat rose before my mind's eye as it must be comparatively rising to his. I, suspected murderer, dressed as twin to my suspected lover, did not delight either his steady or wayward eye, both of which were giving me what's called the fish eye for its glaucous coldness. Still, I tried to make him see the truth. I said, "It is true about Lily. She's set it up so you wouldn't believe her. Or me. Or Wade or anyone."

"You're really low, Morrison," he said, forgetting himself and speaking personally, not officially, "trying to put the blame on a lovely woman like that who says she's been like a mother to you." He shook his head as though he who had experienced all the scum of the earth had now hit bottom mud. "True slime," he muttered.

I turned around and followed Wade out, which is what I should have done in the first place. I tried to walk tall and proud—in a way that didn't look slimy. I would never skulk again. Life is everywhere too short.

Wade was waiting in the van and so was Lia. Apparently, she'd crawled in when we were at the beach and fallen asleep in the back, where Wade kept such a jumble of stuff we'd never noticed her. Wade was laughing. "Lia just told me that she has a friend who's a Gypsy fortune-teller. Crystal ball and all that. This Gypsy told Lia her friend was in big trouble and she would have to talk to save her. Lia thought the Gypsy meant she had to talk like she did, in the same accent. What's the matter?"

I told Wade the rotten thing the policeman had said, how I was true slime.

"I've often thought that way about you myself." Wade smiled. "You should feel proud that a veteran police officer finds you to be the worst specimen of his career. Maybe his comment could appear on subsequent detectives' reports about you."

"Lia, what should I do now? I'm beginning to think there's no way out of this."

"We go see Rusty," Lia said confidently.

"We do?" I couldn't imagine what that would accomplish. Nor did I want to see him.

"Let's go," Wade said, starting his pathetic van engine and pulling out as if it were a Ferrari, not in the least burning rubber.

Lily had been busy. When we got to the Pacific Heights mansion, where Milton was now home and resting, Rusty told us, Lily had confessed to Milton about the "vitamin shots."

"When she found out about the heroin overdose," Rusty recounted, "it took her a few days to put it all together and see what to do. Also, her thoughts were taken up by Dad's heart trouble. This morning she told Dad all about it. He made her go and give a statement to the police because tonight she's leaving for Europe until things settle down. Tomorrow morning, when he's a little stronger, he'll summon the police and tell them to drop the charges. Dad says he's extremely sorry you've suffered this indignity, Rome, and he'll make it up to you somehow, maybe financially, once the will is settled."

"He knows what he can do with his money," I said belligerently.

Wade laughed. "It's not going to be his money to do anything with. If Lily administered the heroin, it's an accidental death, not suicide, and the holograph will stands. Ha!"

"Rome, I'm sorry," Rusty said. "My not believing you must have added to your suffering. Forgive me."

"Of course I will." My heart surged with hope. "Does it mean . . . ?" I was going to ask if knowing I was innocent changed our situation, made him love me again and be engaged to me. I was smiling and beginning to reach toward him as I spoke, but at that moment he turned away as if, having delivered his apology, there was nothing more to say. Lia and Wade both linked their arms in mine and quick-stepped me away. I looked over my shoulder at Rusty, but he didn't notice. His back was still turned.

"Shape up," Wade said. "You're free. Let's celebrate!"

"We go drinka the rum," Lia said.

"And you shape up too," Wade demanded. "Can the stupid accent. Enough's enough."

"Okay. I'll talk like you guys."

TWENTY

The charges against me were dropped. Mrs. D's death was officially declared to be an accidental overdose, which meant the will was settled in favor of Wade. Milton did not take him to court.

Wade kept Milton on as titular head of the Rose Department Store and promised him a (modified) salary as long as he kept away from the place. Milton gave up the mansion and moved to Lily's apartment to await her return from Europe but, wondered I, would she hurry home to marry a man living off the kindness of his stepson?

"Why are you being so nice to Milton?" I asked Wade.

"I feel sorry for him. He's lost Mom, the money, and probably Lily. All he's got now is a bad heart."

It was a month later. We were in Wade's new house on Russian Hill, pretty much the same neighborhood but higher up, with a view of the Bay and more rooms, in one of which lived Lia, who was having private tutoring to get ready for high school in the fall. She would enter as a freshman and try to catch up. Her I.Q. was low and her emotional problems had retarded her intellectual development, but there was no reason she couldn't hope for a normal, useful life, whatever that was. I believed her to be gifted and knew her to be sweet.

She still carried on her own intricate life, no longer at the

Alhambra fountain but at a new bailiwick in the small, tucked-away Russian Hill park I'd found to lunch in that day I fell asleep on the similarly tiled bench. Wade was teaching her to drive.

I had a basement apartment in North Beach, small, partly underground, but warm and cozy and all my own. I called it the coal bin since that's what I think was its heritage, being right next to the building's furnace room. I worked on my novel every day but still worked half days for Wade. When I came home, my writing was out waiting for me, as were all my open books.

Wade and I were lovers. Now, instead of wearing Mother's clothes, I mostly wore Wade's, even some of the brightly colored ones. I was putting on weight and my face was less pallid.

Wade's career was flourishing, but I wondered why he never gave me work to do on the play. Finally, I asked him, "Aren't you going to finish it?"

"No, it's too sad."

"Yes, it is sad, but you needn't be so tied to truth. You can tell it any way you want. Are you referring to the love triangle between Milton, Lily, and your mother?"

"No, I mean the story of the two brothers. Don't forget that's what the play was really all about."

"Yes. The good brother and the bad brother."

"It turned out there was a bad brother and a much worse brother."

I could feel my heart stop and start up again erratically while my skin turned cold, just as it did in the early days of the working on the play.

"Oh, Wade, please, I beg of you, don't let me find out some inexpressibly horrible thing about you just when I . . ."

". . . finally love me?"

230

"Oh, go ahead and tell me," I said grouchily—my old "business voice."

"You already know. It's just that you forgot. Remember the gritty stuff?"

"Gritty stuff?"

We were lying together on his lovely, soft, white, plump sofa. Gone was all the black leather, although he kept the black and white cow picture to which I had pasted on a pink tongue and pink udders.

"Or the strychnine, as you liked to call it. Remember Lia and the packet and all. And how you tried to track down the truth by breaking into my apartment." He laughed, remembering.

I didn't laugh, although I generally did whenever I recollected babooning it through the geraniums, half naked, but at the moment, until I learned what he had in store for me, it was no laughing matter. I was steeled to hear the truth of the two brothers re: the gritty stuff.

He wasn't moving along with the tale, so I helped him. "At the party you poured it into a coffee cup to scare me. But I didn't notice."

"You didn't notice, being too drunk. Mom didn't notice because her back was to me, as was Lily's. Lia noticed because she was helping me. Milton noticed because it was his cup."

"You said it was my cup!"

"That was the play version. This is the real-life dinner party. Milton's cup."

I tried to remember. I was pretty sure it had been my cup in the real-life version, not the play.

Wade continued and I paid attention. "I asked him what he wanted in it, cream or sugar. He said nothing but saw me pour in my little secret packet of something or other, whereupon his eyes practically fell out of his head and he didn't take his eyes off the cup until it was put in front of

231

him. Then, of course, he never touched it. Don't you remember Lily told you about it the night we went to her
apartment together?"

"Yes, but she said it was your mother's cup."

"That was her idea to frighten me off about the will. It
was Milton's cup. I wanted to scare the shit out of him and I
did. I wanted him to see that I knew about him and Lily
and that I hated him for what he was doing to Mom. He got
the message. He knew it wasn't poison. But he couldn't be
sure. Not sure enough to take a sip, at any rate, or even
touch it with his hands."

"Poor Milton. But that's the way the trickster brother
would behave."

"This isn't the play now, Rome. This is the real dinner
party."

"Right." Was it, I wondered dubiously.

"Someone else saw me pour in the little packet."

"Rusty?"

"Yes."

Silence again. Then Wade went on. "Do you remember
what was supposed to happen?"

"He was supposed to get up and take the coffee away and
pour it down the sink and go off into the night and never be
seen again, not ever to know that . . . it was only a trick
you were playing, a mean, nasty joke but not a murder
attempt."

"But Rusty did nothing. He waited for Milton to drink
it. So you see I was the bad brother because I did this
terrible trick but he was the much worse brother because he
didn't know it was a trick and he simply waited to see what
would happen. He hated Milton too."

I knew he didn't. It didn't hold up. Rusty wasn't a hater.
He'd been so good to Milton since his mother's death,
hardly leaving his side. No, this could work for the play but

232

not real life. This must be one more thing Wade was trying on by way of figuring out his life and feelings. Poor Wade.

"Poor Wade," I said aloud. I played along. "You wanted so much to believe in your brother's goodness. But we're all just human, even Rusty."

"Yes, even Rusty. Maybe now it will be easier to love him."

"So it isn't a sad ending. The two alienated brothers can fall into each other's arms at the end."

"No, they can't. Because Rusty will never admit to himself what happened."

"Maybe his ex-fiancée can get him to admit it. He's leaving for Chicago tonight. I didn't want to say good-bye, but now I will. I think it's time he admitted that he was the 'much worse brother' to me too, not sticking by me, not believing in me, and making me feel I was true slime just because I made love to you in your grief when we were both—"

"Insensible at the time," we said in unison.

Wade embraced me, kissed me. "Whatever happens at this farewell scene, don't get engaged again. I need you. I need you to take care of my phone calls when I'm down in L.A."

"Probably all that will happen is that he'll be the gargoyle."

"What's that?"

"Why, it's when he blushes and can't talk and his face twists all up."

"Really?"

I remembered they all used to look away when it happened. Poor Rusty. Poor everyone but me. I could be generous with my sympathy now that I didn't need it all for myself, didn't need any. I was so happy. I had my work, enough money, a lover, and my friends Nancy and Lia.

Nancy was still at the Alhambra, but she didn't need to

233

get another roommate because she was selling art now and making commissions hand over fist. Soon she'd be able to start buying art herself. Hell, soon she'd have her own gallery. She was even writing a column of art criticism for a small city newspaper. She'd got published before me!

She still pined for Rusty, with whom nothing was happening although she managed to see him, at her instigation, for some see-through reason or other that he never saw through. She wasn't going to make an all-out pitch until she felt it was completely over between him and me, which I'd told her it wasn't.

I invited Rusty to the coal bin for a farewell dinner. Upon entering, he smiled at the minuscule space that contained a stove, sink, and refrigerator alongside a flush door set on cement blocks for a desk, above which the windowsills performed as bookshelves. There was a single bed and that, with a bathroom across the hall, was it. For old time's sake I'd painted it green, but my bedcover was a medley of colored flowers and my rug was sheepskin. I had a lot of artificial yellow roses placed hither and thither and lots of different-sized mirrors on the walls to give the illusion of light and space and because they are lucky and pretty and, lastly, because Wade loved catching unexpected looks at himself and I didn't mind seeing more than one of him either.

I loved my place. I had an ongoing soup pot on the stove that I threw different things into each day depending on my finances: sometimes bones and parsley, which I could get for free, sometimes shrimp and asparagus. Tonight, for Rusty, there was chicken, new potatoes, carrots—simmering splendidly in wine and herbed-up broth, being aromatic as hell.

It wasn't until we'd eaten and made a lot of small talk that I brought up the ill-fated engagement party and

Wade's mucking about with the coffee. He said Wade, as usual, was lying and could not be trusted. He said he hadn't seen anything like what I described.

I mulled that over, then asked, "If you had seen it, what would you have done?"

Rusty thought a minute, then said he would probably have gotten up and taken the coffee into the kitchen and thrown it out, just to be on the safe side.

"That's what Wade thought you'd do." I pondered. "What about the watch?" I asked.

"The watch?"

"Remember the night I raided Wade's apartment? When I confronted Wade with Lia's pantomime, you were quick to say it was inspired by a man she'd seen with a pocket watch. That statement has become what is known as a patent lie."

"Yes. I was protecting Wade. But, Rome, why are you questioning me so fiercely? Isn't everything resolved by now?"

"I just want to understand. I guess what I really need to know is why you stopped loving me."

We'd been lounging side by side on the sheepskin rug, leaning against the bed. Now he stood up as if he needed distance to say what he had to say.

"I don't think I ever did love you, Rome. I felt romantic about you. I was feeling vulnerable from the accident and you'd been kind. So incredibly kind." He blushed in a normal way as he said, "I loved the sex. But, because of you, I was getting all enmeshed with the family again, just what I was trying to get away from. Then, when I learned for sure you were involved with Wade, it became impossible. If he had just mistreated you, maybe I could have dealt with it, but when I realized he loved you . . ."

"Do you think he does?" I craned my neck looking up at him. Since the place was so small, he hadn't been able to get very far away to say his say.

"Yes, and probably this coffee-cup scam is an attempt to rub out any last feelings you have for me. I know it must seem unbelievable that Wade, who is so much smarter, handsomer, and successful than I am could be jealous of me, but he is." He turned away as if ashamed.

"That's true. He's said so himself. Because you're so good. Rusty, please sit back down beside me." He did, and I took his hand in mine. "He wants to love you but thinks he can do so only if you'll stop being good." I laughed. "It wasn't enough that you beat up a photographer, you had to not-throw-out Milton's coffee cup even if you didn't see him not-poison it."

Rusty still looked ashamed because I was talking about his benighted goodness. He said sadly, "Maybe I'm good only because I don't love people as ardently as he does. I'm a nice guy only to make up for not being able to love people."

"If that were so, Rusty, if it worked like that, there'd be a lot more nice people than there are."

"I'm sure I didn't hate any of the family. But I know I didn't love any of them."

"Oh, yes, you did. You love them all. Especially Wade. Go to him tonight and tell him you love him."

I could see his spirits lift. Then he said, so sweetly, "What he really needs to hear is that you love him. He says he still hasn't."

I laughed happily. "I'll tell him. And, Rusty"—I kissed him and hugged him—"be a great fireman. Be as happy as you can be and as good as you want to be. Save lives like mad."

"That's my plan. And you can still have your laughing-all-the-time DeRosas."

"I don't know. I hope so. But I've got some books to write first."

And so we parted, Rusty and I, not without a pang on my part. I really had loved him. Probably we would have been a hopeless couple, like Daddy said. What a darling though. I hoped he'd come to grips with being so nice. I hoped he'd never gargoyle up again.

I poured myself a last wine for the day to sip while reading over the morning's writing. Afterward, I tidied up, washed dishes and self, then, stepping from sheepskin to bed, covered myself with flowers, and slept.

At work the next evening, after we made love (the main chore of the day), Wade told me Rusty had come by last night to say good-bye and to say he loved him.

"Did Rusty also tell you he didn't not-throw-out Wade's coffee because he didn't see you not-poison it?"

"Yes."

"Do you believe him?"

"Yes."

"Can you love him anyhow?"

"No."

I laughed. "Try."

"I'll always think you loved him more than me because he's so much more the better man. And you had that incredibly romantic meeting. You sat by his bed. You sang to him. You kissed him awake. It's unforgivable."

"Well, you and I had our scene in the post office. I'd never opened my heart to anyone like I did to you, not even Nancy, and I'd never wept in a man's arms before, not even Daddy's. Plus, you got my virginity."

"Just by a day or two. Speaking of your father, he called you here from Venice. He's eager to get hold of you, says he's got big news."

"Really?" I lit up. "What could it be? Maybe he's coming to visit me."

I called him and got him right away. He told me the news. "Lily's here," he said.

"Oh, really? What's she doing? Running drugs out of a gondola?"

"We've been seeing each other," he said.

"Seeing? What do you mean? Seeing as in . . . ?"

"We're going to be married," he told me.

I was thunderstruck. Like on the day of my arrest when they suddenly said they were taking me down to the station and sashayed into a recital of the Miranda without missing a beat.

Wade, who had sneakily gone to listen in on the other line, now dropped the phone and leapt to my side, putting a sustaining arm around me. That's when I knew I did love him, that he'd always be there with the steadying arm when I turned to jelly, or slime.

"It's probably a bit of a shock, but I know when you think about it, you'll be happy for us," Daddy said. "Lily told me you've always wanted her for a mother. Now she really will be."

"Daddy, this is the woman who let me go to prison for something she had done. And what she had done was true sl—"

"I know," he interrupted. "She explained it all to me. You've both been through a terrible ordeal."

"She hasn't been through anything!" I squealed. "Unless her flight was delayed to Italy. That's her idea of an ordeal, that and having to abandon one millionaire for another. Whereas I went to prison. Then she was going to help me get into an insane asylum as an alternative life-style."

"All right. Stop joking, Rome."

"This isn't a joke. I'm scared for you. She has a heart of iron."

"I'll take my chances."

"She . . ."

"Now, that's enough!" he shouted. Then, more calmly, "The truth is, I've never been so happy."

238

I tried to imagine Daddy with a bounce to his step. It wasn't a pretty picture.

I remembered what he'd said to me that night he cut me off: "You're on your own. I won't help you." I wanted to say the same to him now but I couldn't. It was too cruel. At the time I'd thought he was right to say it, that I'd gone against his wishes and was therefore expendable. Now I knew he wasn't. He'd been cruel. Instead of admitting the truth, I'd let my leg drag. Maybe he had a heart of iron too and they'd be just fine together.

But I wanted to help him. "Daddy, there's no real love or warmth there, no passion. She's not like mother was, or like I am." I stopped. Maybe that sounded good to him.

Daddy was speaking. "She told her story to save you, even though it meant losing Milton and maybe losing all her friends. She's a noble woman. I love her. Good-bye."

I cried. Wade still held me. "There, there," he said, "there, there. It's his life. Let him go. They'll probably be very happy. She was vile to let you go to prison, but it was only for a few days and she was just scared to tell the truth. It's unfortunate, but life is full of misfortunes. That's what life is."

"Wade, maybe love is never real, it's only what you want to believe in. Like Lily. I loved her and thought she loved me, but she was just nice to everyone and I invested her with mother love for me. And Daddy too. I thought he loved me so much but just couldn't express it. It was all a dream. He was fond of me. I think I amused him. But when I was down and out, he didn't know me."

"Rome, it's okay. Because believing someone loves you is almost as good as if they really do. It's the next best thing. And your own feelings of love are real and trustworthy. I think it's great you loved your father so much, because it got you ready to love me."

"I do love you, Wade."

239

"I know. You've loved me from the start."

"And you?"

"I love you just as much as you want to believe I do. And more."

We kissed.

"Aren't you going to drag me out on the balcony and make me watch the sunset?"

I was so surprised by this, I didn't know whether to be horrified or pleased. "Do I do that? No. I'm sure I don't."

"Only on clear evenings. I like it. It teaches me gratitude."

I haven't told Nancy I'm over Rusty and am lovers with Wade. The reason is, I don't want her to go to Chicago. I don't want to lose her. Anyhow, I'm sure Rusty wouldn't have her because it would just make him feel like he was getting enmeshed in the family again. If he did have her, Wade would never let me visit them because he's still so jealous of Rusty, now more than ever because Nurse Wiggin is always going around telling the (real) story of me kissing Rusty (the scion) awake and it eventually got back to Wade. Of course I swore on a stack of Bibles it wasn't true.

On top of that, Wade went to Lia's new bailiwick and caught her latest pantomime. It looks like she's pedaling a unicycle as fast as she can but actually she's being me trampling Wade's jacket so as to get Rusty to make love to me. It just about broke Wade's heart. How did she know? Rusty must have transmitted the information to her one day while they sat silently by the fountain.

I lied myself blue in the face, told Wade Lia had seen a unicycle rider the previous day (the old man-with-the watch subterfuge).

Yes. I still live a life of deceit. It seems to suit a person for whom life is everywhere life and for whom, on most days, there is no tomorrow.

240